THE ENCHANTED TYPEWRITER

John Kendrick Bangs

1st WORLD
LIBRARY
Literary Society

The Enchanted Typewriter

John Kendrick Bangs

© 1st World Library – Literary Society, 2005
PO Box 2211
Fairfield, IA 52556
www.1stworldlibrary.org
First Edition

LCCN: 2005906518

Softcover ISBN: 1-4218-1574-5
Hardcover ISBN: 1-4218-1474-9
eBook ISBN: 1-4218-1674-1

Purchase *"The Enchanted Typewriter"*
as a traditional bound book at:
www.1stWorldLibrary.org/purchase.asp?ISBN=1-4218-1574-5

1st World Library Literary Society is a nonprofit
organization dedicated to promoting literacy by:

- Creating a free internet library accessible from any
  computer worldwide.
- Hosting writing competitions and offering book
  publishing scholarships.

Readers interested in supporting literacy
through sponsorship, donations or
membership please contact:
literacy@1stworldlibrary.org
Check us out at: www.1stworldlibrary.ORG
and start downloading free ebooks today.

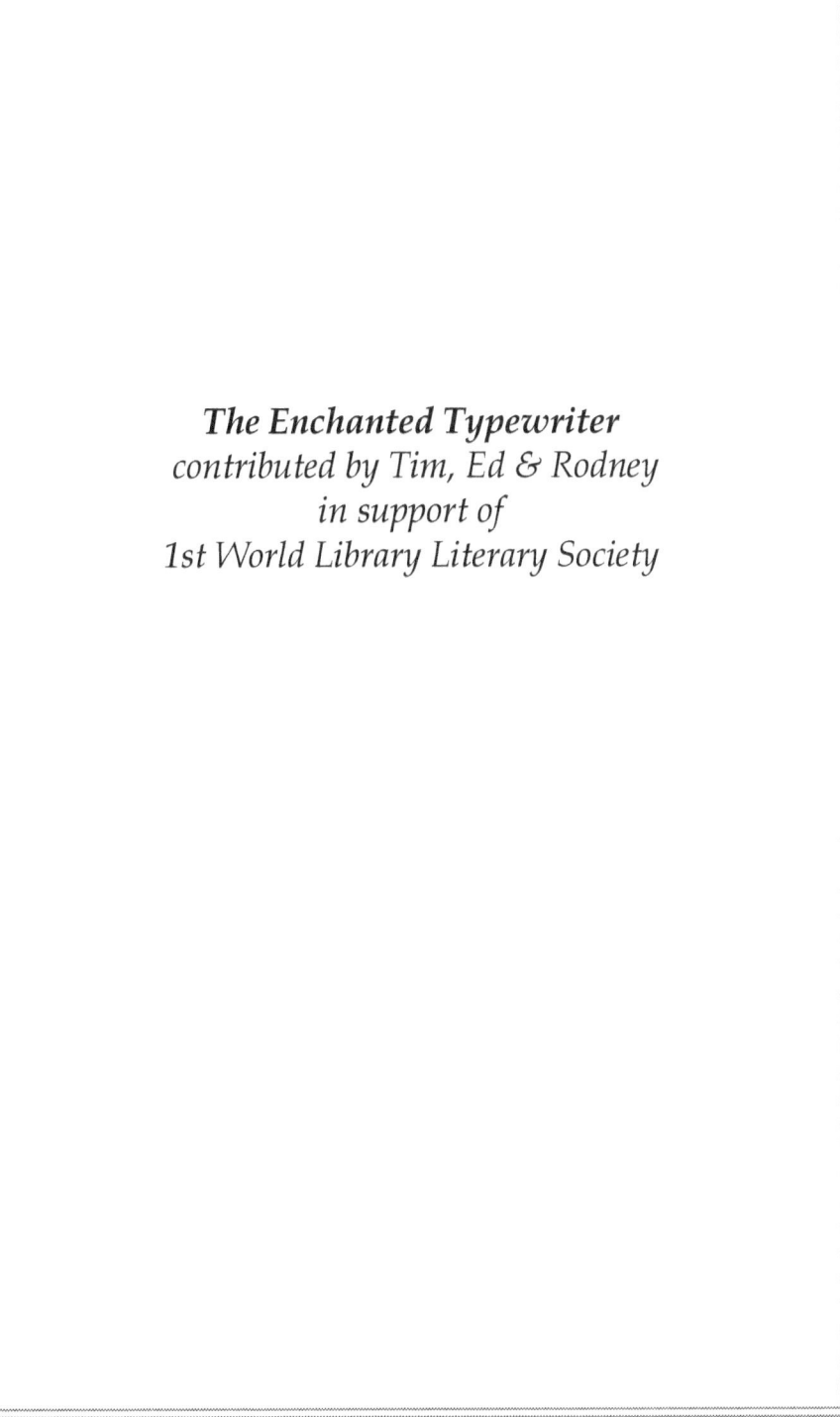

The Enchanted Typewriter
contributed by Tim, Ed & Rodney
in support of
1st World Library Literary Society

I

THE DISCOVERY

It is a strange fact, for which I do not expect ever satisfactorily to account, and which will receive little credence even among those who know that I am not given to romancing - it is a strange fact, I say, that the substance of the following pages has evolved itself during a period of six months, more or less, between the hours of midnight and four o'clock in the morning, proceeding directly from a type-writing machine standing in the corner of my library, manipulated by unseen hands. The machine is not of recent make. It is, in fact, a relic of the early seventies, which I discovered one morning when, suffering from a slight attack of the grip, I had remained at home and devoted my time to pottering about in the attic, unearthing old books, bringing to the light long-forgotten correspondences, my boyhood collections of "stuff," and other memory-inducing things. Whence the machine came originally I do not recall. My impression is that it belonged to a stenographer once in the employ of my father, who used frequently to come to our house to take down dictations. However this may be, the machine had lain hidden by dust and the flotsam and jetsam of the house for twenty years, when, as I have said, I came upon it unexpectedly. Old man as I am - I shall soon be thirty - the fascination of a machine has lost none of its potency. I am as pleased to-day watching the wheels of my watch "go round" as ever I was, and to "monkey" with a type-writing apparatus has always brought great joy into my heart - though for composing give me the pen. Perhaps I should apologize for the use here of the verb monkey, which savors of what a friend of mine calls the "English slanguage," to differentiate it from what he also calls the "Andrew Language." But I shall not do so, because, to whatever branch of our tongue the word may belong, it is exactly descriptive, and descriptive as no other word can be, of what a boy does with things that click and "go," and is therefore not at all out of place in a tale which I trust will be regarded as a polite one.

The discovery of the machine put an end to my attic potterings. I cared little for finding old bill-files and collections of Atlantic cable-ends when, with a whole morning, a type-writing machine, and a screw-driver before me I could penetrate the mysteries of that useful mechanism. I shall not endeavor to describe the delightful sensations of that hour of screwing and unscrewing; they surpass the powers of my pen. Suffice it to say that I took the whole apparatus apart, cleaned it well, oiled every joint, and then put it together again. I do not suppose a seven-year-old boy could have derived more satisfaction from taking a piano to pieces. It was exhilarating, and I resolved that as a reward for the pleasure it had given me the machine should have a brand-new ribbon and as much ink as it could consume. And that, in brief, is how it came to be that this machine of antiquated pattern was added to the library bric-a-brac. To say the truth, it was of no more practical use than Barye's dancing bear, a plaster cast of which adorns my mantel-shelf, so that when I classify it with the bric-a-brac I do so advisedly. I frequently tried to write a jest or two upon it, but the results were extraordinarily like

Sir Arthur Sullivan's experience with the organ into whose depths the lost chord sank, never to return. I dashed off the jests well enough, but somewhere between the keys and the types they were lost, and the results, when I came to scan the paper, were depressing. And once I tried a sonnet on the keys. Exactly how to classify the jumble that came out of it I do not know, but it was curious enough to have appealed strongly to D'Israeli or any other collector of the literary oddity. More singular than the sonnet, though, was the fact that when I tried to write my name upon this strange machine, instead of finding it in all its glorious length written upon the paper, I did find "William Shakespeare" printed there in its stead. Of course you will say that in putting the machine together I mixed up the keys and the letters. I have no doubt that I did, but when I tell you that there have been times when, looking at myself in the glass, I have fancied that I saw in my mirrored face the lineaments of the great bard; that the contour of my head is precisely the same as was his; that when visiting Stratford for the first time every foot of it was pregnant with clearly defined recollections to me, you will perhaps more easily picture to yourself my sensations at the moment.

However, enough of describing the machine in its relation to myself. I have said sufficient, I think, to convince you that whatever its make, its age, and its limitations, it was an extraordinary affair; and, once convinced of that, you may the more readily believe me when I tell you that it has gone into business apparently for itself - and incidentally for me.

It was on the morning of the 26th of March last that I discovered the curious condition of affairs concerning which I have essayed to write. My family do not agree with me as to the date. They say that it was on the evening of the 25th of March that the episode had its beginning; but they are not aware, for I have not told them, that it was not evening, but morning, when I reached home after the dinner at the Aldus Club. It was at a quarter of three A.M. precisely that I entered my house and proceeded to remove my hat and coat, in which operation I was interrupted, and in a startling manner, by a click from the dark recesses of the library. A man does not like to hear a click which he cannot comprehend, even before he has dined. After he has dined, however, and feels a satisfaction with life which cannot come to him before dinner, to hear a mysterious click, and from a dark corner, at an hour when the world is at rest, is not pleasing. To say that my heart jumped into my mouth is mild. I believe it jumped out of my mouth and rebounded against the wall opposite back though my system into my boots. All the sins of my past life, and they are many - I once stepped upon a caterpillar, and I have coveted my neighbor both his man-servant and his maid-servant, though not his wife nor his ass, because I don't like his wife and he keeps no live-stock - all my sins, I say, rose up before me, for I expected every moment that a bullet would penetrate my brain, or my heart if perchance the burglar whom I suspected of levelling a clicking revolver at me aimed at my feet.

"Who is there?" I cried, making a vocal display of bravery I did not feel, hiding behind our hair sofa.

The only answer was another click.

"This is serious," I whispered softly to myself. "There are two of 'em; I am in the light, unarmed. They are concealed by the darkness and have revolvers. There is only one way out of this, and that is by strategy. I'll pretend I think I've made a mistake." So I addressed myself aloud.

"What an idiot you are," I said, so that my words could be heard by the burglars. "If this is the effect of Aldus Club dinners you'd better give them up. That click wasn't a click at all, but the ticking of our new eight-day clock."

I paused, and from the corner there came a dozen more clicks in quick succession, like the cocking of as many revolvers.

"Great Heavens!" I murmured, under my breath. "It must be Ali Baba with his forty thieves."

As I spoke, the mystery cleared itself, for following close upon a thirteenth click came the gentle ringing of a bell, and I knew then that the type-writing machine was in action; but this was by no means a reassuring discovery. Who or what could it be that was engaged upon the type-writer at that unholy hour, 3 A.M.? If a mortal being, why was my coming no interruption? If a super-natural being, what infernal complication might not the immediate future have in store for me?

My first impulse was to flee the house, to go out into the night and pace the fields - possibly to rush out to the golf links and play a few holes in the dark in order to cool my brow, which was rapidly becoming fevered. Fortunately, however, I am not a man of impulse. I never yield to a mere nerve suggestion, and so, instead of going out into the storm and certainly contracting pneumonia, I walked boldly into the library to investigate the causes of the very extraordinary incident. You may rest well assured, however, that I took care to go armed, fortifying myself with a stout stick, with a long, ugly steel blade concealed within it - a cowardly weapon, by-the-way, which I permit to rest in my house merely because it forms a part of a collection of weapons acquired through the failure of a comic paper to which I had contributed several articles. The editor, when the crash came, sent me the collection as part payment of what was owed me, which I think was very good of him, because a great many people said that it was my stuff that killed the paper. But to return to the story. Fortifying myself with the sword-cane, I walked boldly into the library, and, touching the electric button, soon had every gas-jet in the room giving forth a brilliant flame; but these, brilliant as they were, disclosed nothing in the chair before the machine.

The latter, apparently oblivious of my presence, went clicking merrily and as rapidly along as though some expert young woman were in charge. Imagine the situation if you can. A type-writing machine of ancient make, its letters clear, but out of accord with the keys, confronted by an empty chair, three hours after midnight, rattling off page after page of something which might or might not be readable, I could not at the moment determine. For two or three minutes I gazed in open-mouthed wonder. I was not frightened, but I did experience a sensation which comes from contact with the uncanny. As I gradually grasped the situation and became used, somewhat, to what was going on, I ventured a remark.

"This beats the deuce!" I observed.

The machine stopped for an instant. The sheet of paper upon which the impressions of letters were being made flew out from under the cylinder, a pure white sheet was as quickly substituted, and the keys clicked off the line:

"What does?"

I presumed the line was in response to my assertion, so I replied:

"You do. What uncanny freak has taken possession of you to-night that you start in to write on your own hook, having resolutely declined to do any writing for me ever since I rescued you from the dust and dirt and cobwebs of the attic?"

"You never rescued me from any attic," the machine replied. "You'd better go to bed; you've dined too well, I imagine. When did you rescue me from the dust and dirt and the cobwebs of any attic?"

"What an ungrateful machine you are!" I cried. "If you have sense enough to go into writing on your own account, you ought to have mind enough to remember the years you spent up-stairs under the roof neglected, and covered with hammocks, awnings, family portraits, and receipted bills."

"Really, my dear fellow," the machine tapped back, "I must repeat it. Bed is the place for you. You're not coherent. I'm not a machine, and upon my honor, I've never seen your darned old attic."

"Not a machine!" I cried. "Then what in Heaven's name are you? - a sofa-cushion?"

"Don't be sarcastic, my dear fellow," replied the machine. "Of course I'm not a machine; I'm Jim - Jim Boswell."

"What?" I roared. "You? A thing with keys and type and a bell -"

"I haven't got any keys or any type or a bell. What on earth are you talking about?" replied the machine. "What have you been eating?"

"What's that?" I asked, putting my hand on the keys.

"That's keys," was the answer.

"And these, and that?" I added, indicating the type and the bell.

"Type and bell," replied the machine.

"And yet you say you haven't got them," I persisted.

"No, I haven't. The machine has got them, not I," was the response. "I'm not the machine. I'm the man that's using it - Jim - Jim Boswell. What good would a bell do me? I'm not a cow or a bicycle. I'm the editor of the Stygian Gazette, and I've come here to copy off my notes of what I see and hear, and besides all this I do type-writing for various people in Hades, and as this machine of yours seemed to be of no use to you I thought I'd try it. But if you object, I'll go."

As I read these lines upon the paper I stood amazed and delighted.

"Go!" I cried, as the full value of his patronage of my machine dawned upon me, for I could sell his copy and he would be none the worse off, for, as I understand the copyright laws, they are not designed to benefit authors, but for the protection of type-setters. "Why, my dear fellow, it would break my heart if, having found my machine to your taste, you should ever think of using another. I'll lend you my bicycle, too, if you'd like it - in fact, anything I have is at your command."

"Thank you very much," returned Boswell through the medium of the keys, as usual. "I shall not need your bicycle, but this machine is of great value to me. It has several very remarkable qualities which I have never found in any other machine. For instance, singular to relate, Mendelssohn and I were fooling about here the other night, and when he saw this machine he thought it was a spinet of some new pattern; so what does he do but sit down and play me one of his songs without words on it, and, by jove! when he got through, there was the theme of the whole thing printed on a sheet of paper before him."

"You don't really mean to say -" I began.

"I'm telling you precisely what happened," said Boswell. "Mendelssohn was tickled to death with it, and he played every song without words that he ever wrote, and every one of 'em was fitted with words which he said absolutely conveyed the ideas he meant to bring out with the music. Then I tried the machine, and discovered another curious thing about it. It's intensely American. I had a story of Alexander Dumas' about his Musketeers that he wanted translated from French into American, which is the language we speak below, in preference to German, French, Volapuk, or English. I thought I'd copy off a few lines of the French original, and as true as I'm sitting here before your eyes, where you can't see me, the copy I got was a good, though rather free, translation. Think of it! That's an advanced machine for you!"

I looked at the machine wistfully. "I wish I could make it work," I said; and I tried as before to tap off my name, and got instead only a confused jumble of letters. It wouldn't even pay me the compliment of transforming my name into that of Shakespeare, as it had previously done.

It was thus that the magic qualities of the machine were made known to me, and out of it the following papers have grown. I have set them down without much editing or alteration, and now submit them to your inspection, hoping that in perusing them you will derive as much satisfaction and delight as I have in being the possessor of so wonderful a machine, manipulated by so interesting a person as "Jim - Jim Boswell" - as he always calls himself - and others, who, as you will note, if perchance you have the patience to read further, have upon occasions honored my machine by using it.

I must add in behalf of my own reputation for honesty that Mr. Boswell has given me all right, title, and interest in these papers in this world as a return for my permission to him to use my machine.

"What if they make a hit and bring in barrels of gold in royalties," he said. "I can't take it back with me where I live, so keep it yourself."

II

MR. BOSWELL IMPARTS SOME
LATE NEWS OF HADES

Boswell was a little late in arriving the next night. He had agreed to be on hand exactly at midnight, but it was after one o'clock before the machine began to click and the bell to ring. I had fallen asleep in the soft upholstered depths of my armchair, feeling pretty thoroughly worn out by the experiences of the night before, which, in spite of their pleasant issue, were nevertheless somewhat disturbing to a nervous organization like mine. Suddenly I waked, and with the awakening there entered into my mind the notion that the whole thing was merely a dream, and that in the end it would be the better for me if I were to give up Aldus and other club dinners with nightmare inducing menus. But I was soon convinced that the real state of affairs was quite otherwise, and that everything really had happened as I have already related it to you, for I had hardly gotten my eyes free from what my poetic son calls "the seeds of sleep" when I heard the type-writer tap forth:

"Hello, old man!"

Incidentally let me say that this had become another interesting feature of the machine. Since my first interview with Boswell the taps seemed to speak, and if some one were sitting before it and writing a line the mere differentiation of sounds of the various keys would convey to the mind the ideas conveyed to it by the printed words. So, as I say, my ears were greeted with a clicking "Hello, old man!" followed immediately by the bell.

"You are late," said I, looking at my watch.

"I know it," was the response. "But I can't help it. During the campaign I am kept so infernally busy I hardly know where I am."

"Campaign, eh?" I put in. "Do you have campaigns in Hades?"

"Yes," replied Boswell, "and we are having a - well, to be polite, a regular Gehenna of a time. Things have changed much in Hades latterly. There has been a great growth in the democratic spirit below, and his Majesty is having a deuce of a time running his kingdom. Washington and Cromwell and Caesar have had the nerve to demand a constitution from the venerable Nicholas -"

"From whom?" I queried, perplexed somewhat, for I was not yet fully awake.

"Old Nick," replied Boswell; "and I can tell you there's a pretty fight on between the supporters of the administration and the opposition. Secure in his power, the Grand Master of Hades has been somewhat arbitrary, and he has made the mistake of doing some of his subjects a little too brown. Take the case of Bonaparte, for instance: the government has ruled that he was personally responsible for all the wars of Europe from 1800 up to Waterloo, and it was proposed to hang him once for every man killed on either side throughout that period. Bonaparte naturally resisted. He said he had a good neck, which he did not object to have broken three or four times, because he admitted he deserved it; but when it came to hanging him five or six million times, once a month, for, say, five million months, or twelve times a year for 415,000 years, he didn't like it, and wouldn't stand it, and wanted to submit the question to arbitration.

"Nicholas observed that the word arbitration was not in his especially expurgated dictionary, whereupon Bonaparte remarked that he wasn't responsible for that; that he thought it a good word and worthy of incorporation in any dictionary and in all vocabularies.

"'I don't care what you think,' retorted his Majesty. 'It's what I don't think that goes;' and he commanded his imps to prepare the gallows on the third Thursday of each month for Bonaparte's expiation; ordered his secretary to send Bonaparte a type-written notice that his presence on each occasion was expected, and gave orders to the police to see that he was there willy-nilly. Naturally Bonaparte resisted, and appealed to the courts. Blackstone sustained his appeal, and Nicholas overruled him. The first Thursday came, and the police went for the Emperor, but he was surrounded by a good half of the men who had fought under him, and the minions of the law could do nothing against them. In consequence, Bonaparte's brother, Joseph, a quiet, inoffensive citizen, was dragged from his home and hanged in his place, Nicholas contending that when a soldier could not, or would not, serve, the government had a right to expect a substitute. Well," said Boswell, at this point, "that set all Hades on fire. We were divided as to Bonaparte's deserts, but the hanging of other people as substitutes was too much. We didn't know who'd be substituted next. The English backed up Blackstone, of course. The French army backed up Bonaparte. The inoffensive citizens were aroused in behalf of Joseph, for they saw at once whither they were drifting if the substitute idea was carried out to its logical conclusion; and in half an hour the administration was on the defensive, which, as you know, is a very, very, very bad thing for an administration."

"It is, if it desires to be returned to office," said I.

"It is anyhow," replied Boswell through the medium of the keys. "It's in exactly the same position as that of a humorist who has to print explanatory diagrams with all of his jokes. The administration papers were hot over the situation. The king can do no wrong idea was worked for all it was worth, but beyond this they drew pathetic pictures of the result of all these deplorable tendencies. What was Hades for, they asked, if a man, after leading a life of crime in the other world, was not to receive his punishment there? The attitude of the opposition was a radical and vicious blow at the vital principles of the sphere itself. The opposition papers coolly and calmly took the position that the vital principles of Hades were all right; that it was the extreme view as to the power of the Emperor taken by that person himself that wouldn't go in these democratic days. Punishment for Bonaparte was the correct thing, and Bonaparte expected some, but was not grasping enough to want it all. They added that recent fully settled ideas as to a humane application of the laws required the bunching of the indictments or the selection of one and a fair trial based upon that, and that anyhow, under no circumstances, should a wholly innocent person be made to suffer for the crimes of another. These journals were suppressed, but the next day a set of new papers were started to promulgate the same theories as to individual rights. The province of Cimmeria declared itself independent of the throne, and set up in the business of government for itself. Gehenna declared for the Emperor, but insisted upon home rule for cities of its own class, and finally, as I informed you at the beginning, Washington, Cromwell, and Caesar went in person to Apollyon and demanded a constitution. That was the day before yesterday, and just what will come of it we don't as yet know, because Washington and Cromwell and Caesar have not been seen since, but we have great fears for them, because seventeen car-loads of vitriol and a thousand extra tons of coal were ordered by the Lord High Steward of the palace to be delivered to the Minister of Justice last night."

"Quite a complication," said I. "The Americanization of Hades has begun at last. How does society regard the affair?"

"Variously," observed Boswell. "Society hates the government as much as anybody, and really believes in curtailing the Emperor's powers, but, on the other hand, it desires to maintain all of its own aristocratic privileges. The main trouble in Hades at present is the gradual disintegration of society; that is to say, its former component parts are beginning to differentiate them- selves the one from the other."

"Like capital and labor here?" I queried.

"In a sense, yes - possibly more like your Colonial Dames, and Daughters of the Revolution. For instance, great organizations are in process of formation - people are beginning to flock together for purposes of protection. Charles the First and Henry the Eighth and

Louis the Fourteenth have established Ye Ancient and Honorable Order of Kings, to which only those who have actually worn crowns shall be eligible. The painters have gotten together with a Society of Fine Arts, the sculptors have formed a Society of Chisellers, and all the authors from Homer down to myself have got up an Authors' Club where we have a lovely time talking about ourselves, no man to be eligible who hasn't written something that has lasted a hundred years. Perhaps, if you are thinking of coming over soon, you'll let me put you on our waiting-list?"

I smiled at his seeming inconsistency and let myself into his snare.

"I haven't written anything that has lasted a hundred years yet," said I.

"Oh, yes, I think you have," replied Boswell, and the machine seemed to laugh as he wrote out his answer. "I saw a joke of yours the other day that's two hundred centuries old. Diogenes showed it to me and said that it was a great favorite with his grandfather, who had inherited it from one of his remote ancestors."

A hot retort was on my lips, but I had no wish to offend my guest, so I smiled and observed that I had frequently indulged in unconscious plagiarism of that sort.

"I should imagine," I hastened to add, "that to men like Charles the First this uncertainty as to the safety of Cromwell would be great joy."

"I hardly know," returned Boswell. "That very question has been discussed among us. Charles made a great outward show of grief when he heard of the coal being delivered at the office of the Minister of Justice, and we all thought him quite magnanimous, but it leaked out, just before I left to come here, that he sent his private secretary to the palace with a Panama hat and a palm-leaf fan for Cromwell, with his congratulations.

"That seems to savor somewhat of sarcasm."

"Oh, ultimately Hades is bound to be a republic," replied Boswell. "There are too many clever and ambitious politicians among us for the place to go along as a despotism much longer. If the place were filled up with poets and society people, and things like that, it might go on as an autocracy forever, but you see it isn't. To men of the caliber of Alexander the Great and Bonaparte and Caesar, and a thousand other warriors who never were used to taking orders from anybody, but were themselves headquarters, the despotic sway of Apollyon is intolerable, and he hasn't made any effort to conciliate any of them. If he had appointed Bonaparte commander-in-chief of his army and made a friend of him, instead of ordering him to be hanged every month for 415,000 years, or put Caesar in as Secretary of State, instead of having him roasted three times a month for seventy or eighty centuries, he would have strengthened his hold. As it is, he has ignored all these people officially, treats them like criminals personally; makes friends with Mazarin and Powhatan, awards the office of Tax Assessor to Dick Turpin, and makes old Falstaff commander of his Imperial Guard. And just because poor Ben Jonson scribbled off a rhyme for my paper, The Gazette - a rhyme running:

Mazarin And Powhatan,
Turpin and Falstaff,
Form, you bet, A cabinet

To make a donkey laugh.

Mazarin And Powhatan
Run Apollyon's state.
The Dick and Jacks Collect the tax -
The people pay the freight.

- just because Jonson wrote that and I published it, my paper was confiscated, Jonson was boiled in oil for ten weeks, and I was seized and thrown into a dungeon where a lot of savages from the South Sea Islands tattooed the darned old jingle between my shoulder blades in green letters, and not satisfied with this barbaric act, right under the jingle they added the line, in red letters, 'This edition strictly limited to one copy, for private circulation only,' and they every one of 'em, Apollyon, Mazarin, and the rest, signed the guarantee personally with red-hot pens dipped in sulphuric acid. It makes a valuable collection of autographs, no doubt, but I prefer my back as nature made it. Talk about enlightened government under a man who'll permit things like that to be done!"

I ought not to have done it, but I couldn't help smiling.

"I must say," I observed, apologetically, "that the treatment was barbarous, but really I do think it showed a sense of humor on the part of the government."

"No doubt," replied Boswell, with a sigh; "but when the joke is on me I don't enjoy it very much. I'm only human, and should prefer to observe that the government had some sense of justice."

The apparently empty chair before the machine gave a slight hitch forward, and the type-writer began to tap again.

"You'll have to excuse me now," observed Boswell through the usual medium. "I have work to do, and if you'll go to bed like a good fellow, while I copy off the minutes of the last meeting of the Authors' Club, I'll see that you don't lose anything by it. After I get the minutes done I have an interesting story for my Sunday paper from the advance sheets of Munchausen's Further Recollections, which I shall take great pleasure in leaving for you when I depart. If you will take the bundle of manuscript I leave with you and boil it in alcohol for ten minutes, you will be able to read it, and, no doubt, if you copy it off, sell it for a goodly sum. It is guaranteed absolutely genuine."

"Very well," said I, rising, "I'll go; but I should think you would put in most of your time whacking at the government editorially, instead of going in for minutes and abstract stories of adventure."

"You do, eh?" said Boswell. "Well, if you were in my place you'd change your mind. After my unexpected endorsement by the Emperor and his cabinet, I've decided to keep out of politics for a little while. I can stand having a poem tattooed on my back, but if it came to having a three-column editorial expressing my emotions etched alongside of my spine, I'm afraid I'd disappear into thin air."

So I left him at work and retired. The next morning I found the promised bundle of manuscripts, and, after boiling the pages as instructed, discovered the following tale.

III

FROM ADVANCE SHEETS OF BARON MUNCHAUSEN'S FURTHER RECOLLECTIONS

It is with some very considerable hesitation that I come to this portion of my personal recollections, and yet I feel that I owe it to my fellow-citizens in this delightful Stygian country, where we are all enjoying our well-earned rest, to lay before them the exact truth concerning certain incidents which have now passed into history, and for participation in which a number of familiar figures are improperly gaining all the credit, or discredit, as the case may be. It is not a pleasant task to expose an impostor; much less is it agreeable to expose four impostors; but to one who from the earliest times - and when I say earliest times I speak advisedly, as you will see as you read on - to one, I say, who from the earliest times has been actuated by no other motive than the promulgation of truth, the task of exposing fraud becomes a duty which cannot be ignored. Therefore, with regret I set down this chapter of my memoirs, regardless of its consequences to certain figures which have been of no inconsiderable importance in our community for many years - figures which in my own favorite club, the Associated Shades, have been most welcome, but which, as I and they alone know, have been nothing more than impostures.

In previous volumes I have confined my attention to my memoirs as Baron Munchausen - but, dear reader, there are others. I WAS NOT ALWAYS BARON MUNCHAUSEN; I HAVE BEEN OTHERS! I am not aware that it has fallen to the lot of any but myself in the whole span of universal existence to live more than one life upon that curious, compact little ball of land and water called the Earth, but, in any event, to me has fallen that privilege or distinction, or whatever it may be, and upon the record made by me in four separate existences, placed centuries apart, four residents of this sphere are basing their claims to notice, securing election to our clubs, and even venturing so far at times as to make themselves personally obnoxious to me, who with a word could expose their wicked deceit in all its naked villainy to an astounded community. And in taking this course they have gone too far. There is a limit beyond which no man shall dare go with me. Satisfied with the ultimate embodiment of my virtues in the Baron Munchausen, I have been disposed to allow the impostors to pursue their deception in peace so long as they otherwise behave themselves, but when Adam chooses to allude to my writings as frothy lies, when Jonah attacks my right as a literary person to tell tales of leviathans, when Noah states that my ignorance in yachting matters is colossal, and when William Shakespeare publicly brands me as a person unworthy of belief who should be expelled from the Associated Shades, then do I consider it time to speak out and expose four of the greatest frauds that have ever been inflicted upon a long-suffering public.

To begin at the beginning then, let me state that my first recollection dates back to a beautiful summer morning, when in a lovely garden I opened my eyes and became conscious of two very material facts: first, a charming woman arranging her hair in the mirror-like waters of a silver lake directly before me; and, second, a poignant pain in my side, as though I had been operated upon for appendicitis, but which in reality resulted from the loss of a rib which had in turn evoluted into the charming and very human being I now saw before me. That woman was Eve; that mirror-like lake was set in the midst of the Garden of Eden; I was Adam, and not this watery-eyed antediluvian calling himself by my name, who is a familiar figure in the Anthropological Society, an authority on evolution, and a blot upon civilization.

I have little to say about this first existence of mine. It was full of delights. Speech not having been invented, Eve was an attractive companion to a man burdened as I was with responsibilities, and until our children were born we went our way in happiness and silence. It is not in the nature of things, however, that children should not wish to talk, and it was through the irrepressible efforts of Cain and Abel to be heard as well as seen that first called the attention of Eve and myself to the desirability of expressing our thoughts in words rather than by masonic signs.

I shall not burden my readers with further recollections of this period. It was excessively primitive, of necessity, but before leaving it I must ask the reader to put one or two questions to himself in this matter.

1st. How is it that this bearded patriarch, who now poses as the only original Adam, has never been able, with any degree of positiveness, to answer the question as to whether or not he was provided with a caudal appendage - a question which I am prepared to answer definitely, at any moment, if called upon by the proper authorities, and, if need be, to produce not only the tail itself, but the fierce and untamed pterodactyl that bit it off upon that unfortunate autumn afternoon when he and I had our first and last conflict.

2d. Why is it that when describing a period concerning which he is supposed to know all, he seems to have given voice to sentiments in phrases which would have delighted Sheridan and shed added glory upon the eloquence of Webster, AT A TIME WHEN, AS I HAVE ALREADY SHOWN, THERE WAS NO SUCH THING AS SPEECH?

Upon these two points alone I rest my case against Adam: the first is the reticence of guilt - he doesn't know, and he knows he doesn't know; the second is a deliberate and offensive prevarication, which shows again that he doesn't know, and assumes that we are all equally ignorant.

So much for Adam. Now for the cheap and year-ridden person who has taken unto himself my second personality, Noah; and that other strange combination of woe and wickedness, Jonah, who has chosen to pre-empt my third. I shall deal with both at one and the same time, for, taken separately, they are not worthy of notice.

Noah asserts that I know nothing of yachting. I will accept the charge with the qualification that I know a great sight more about Arking than he does; and as for Jonah, I can give Jonah points on whaling, and I hereby challenge them both to a Memoir Match for $2000 a side, in gold, to see which can give to the world the most interesting reminiscences concerning the cruises of the two craft in question, the Ark and the Whale, upon neither of which did either of these two anachronisms ever set foot, and of both of which I, in my two respective existences, was commander-in-chief. The fact is that, as in the case of the fictitious Adam, these two impersonators are frauds. The man now masquerading as Noah was my hired man in the latter part of the antediluvian period; was discharged three years before the flood; was left on shore at the hour of departure, and when last seen by me was sitting on the top of an apple-tree, begging to do two men's work for nothing if we'd only let him out of the wet. If he will at any time submit to a cross-examination at my hands as to the principal events of that memorable voyage, I will show to any fair-minded judge how impossible is his claim that he was in command, or even afloat, after the first week. I have hitherto kept silent in this matter, in spite of many and repeated outrageous flings, for the sake of his - or rather my - family, who have been deceived, as have all the rest of us, barring, of course, myself. References to portraits of leading citizens of that period will easily show how this can be. We were all alike as two peas in the olden days, and at a time when men reached to an advanced age which is not known now, it frequently became almost impossible to distinguish one old man from another. I will say, finally, in regard to this person Noah that if he can give to the public a statement telling the essential differences between a pterodactyl and a double spondee that will not prove utterly absurd to an educated person, I will withdraw my accusation and resign from the club. BUT I KNOW WELL HE CANNOT DO IT, and he does too, and that is about the extent of his knowledge.

Now as to Jonah. I really dislike very much to tread upon this worthy's toes, and I should not do it had he not chosen to clap an injunction upon a volume of Tales of the Whales, which I wrote for children last summer, claiming that I was infringing upon his copyright, and feeling that I as a self-respecting man would never claim the discredit of having myself been the person he claims to have been. I will candidly confess that I am not proud of my achievements as Jonah. I was a very oily person even before I embarked upon the seas as Lord High Admiral of H.M.S. Leviathan. I was not a pleasant person to know. If I spent the night with a friend, his roof would fall in or his house would burn down. If I bet on a horse, he would lead up to the home-stretch and fall down dead an inch from the finish. If I went into a stock speculation, I was invariably caught on a rising or a falling market. In my youth I spoiled every yachting-party I went on by attracting a gale. When I came out the moon went behind a cloud, and people who began by endorsing my paper ended up in the poor-house. Commerce wouldn't have me. Boards of Trade everywhere repudiated me, and I gradually sank into that state of despair which finds no solace anywhere but on the sea or in politics, and as politics was then unknown I went to sea. The result is known to the world. I was cast overboard, ingulfed by a whale, which, in his defence let me be generous enough to say, swallowed me inadvertently and with the usual result. I came back, and life went on. Finally I came here, and when it got to the ears of the authorities that I was in Hades, they sent me back for the fourth time to earth in the person of William Shakespeare.

That is the whole of the Jonah story. It is a sad story, and I regret it; and I am sorry for the impostor when I reflect that the character he has assumed possesses attractions for him. His real life must have been a fearful thing if he is happy in his impersonation, and for his punishment let us leave him where he is. Having told the truth, I have done my duty. I cheerfully resign my claim to the personality he claims - I relinquish from this time on all right, title, and interest in the name; but if he ever dares to interfere with me again in the use of my personal recollections concerning the inside of whales I shall hale him before the authorities.

And now, finally, I come to Shakespeare, whom I have kept for the last, not because he was the last chronologically, but because I like to work up to a climax.

Previous to my existence as Baron Munchausen I lived for a term of years on earth as William Shakespeare, and what I have to say now is more in the line of confession than otherwise.

In my boyhood I was wild and I poached. If I were not afraid of having it set down as a joke, I should say that I poached everything from eggs to deer. I was not a great joy to my parents. There was no deviltry in Stratford in which I did not take a leading part, and finally, for the good of Warwickshire, I was sent to London, where a person of my talents was more likely to find congenial and appreciative surroundings. A glance at such of my autographs as are now extant will demonstrate the fact that I never learned to write; a glance at the first folios of the plays attributed to me will likewise show that I never learned to spell; and yet I walked into London with one of the most exquisite poems in the English language in my pocket. I am still filled with merriment over it. How was it, the critics of the years since have asked - how was it that this untutored little savage from leafy Warwickshire, with no training and little education, came into London with "Venus and Adonis" in manuscript in his pocket? It is quite evident that the critic fraternity have no Sherlock Holmes in their midst. It would not take much of an eye, a true detective's eye, to see the milk in that cocoanut, for it is but a simple tale after all. The way of it was this: On my way from

Stratford to London I walked through Coventry, and I remained in Coventry overnight. I was ill-clad and hungry, and, having no money with which to pay for my supper, I went to the Royal Arms Hotel and offered my services as porter for the night, having noted that a rich cavalcade from London, en route to Kenilworth, had arrived unexpectedly at the Royal Arms. Taken by surprise, and, therefore, unprepared to accommodate so many guests, the landlord was glad to avail himself of my services, and I was assigned to the position of boots. Among others whom I served was Walter Raleigh, who, noting my ragged condition and hearing what a roisterer and roustabout I had been, immediately took pity upon me, and gave me a plum-colored court-suit with which he was through, and which I accepted, put upon my back, and next day wore off to London. It was in the pocket of this that I found the poem of "Venus and Adonis." That poem, to keep myself from starving, I published when I reached London, sending a compli- mentary copy of course to my benefactor. When Raleigh saw it he was naturally surprised but gratified, and on his return to London he sought me out, and suggested the publication of his sonnets. I was the first man he'd met, he said, who was willing to publish his stuff on his own responsibility. I immediately put out some of the sonnets, and in time was making a comfortable living, publishing the anonymous works of most of the young bucks about town, who paid well for my imprint. That the public chose to think the works were mine was none of my fault. I never claimed them, and the line on the title-page, "By William Shakespeare," had reference to the publisher only, and not, as many have chosen to believe, to the author. Thus were published Lord Bacon's "Hamlet," Raleigh's poems, several plays of Messrs. Beaumont and Fletcher - who were themselves among the cleverest adapters of the times - and the rest of that glorious monument to human credulity and memorial to an impossible, wholly apocryphal genius, known as the works of William Shakespeare. The extent of my writing during this incarnation was ten autographs for collectors, and one attempt at a comic opera called "A Midsummer's Nightmare," which was never produced, because no one would write the music for it, and which was ultimately destroyed with three of my quatrains and all of Bacon's evidence against my authorship of "Hamlet," in the fire at the Globe Theatre in the year 1613.

These, then, dear reader, are the revelations which I have to make. In my next incarnation I was the man I am now known to be, Baron Munchausen. As I have said, I make the exposure with regret, but the arrogance of these impudent impersonators of my various personalities has grown too great to be longer borne. I lay the simple story of their villany before you for what it is worth. I have done my duty. If after this exposure the public of Hades choose to receive them in their homes and at their clubs, and as guests at their functions, they will do it with a full knowledge of their duplicity.

In conclusion, fearing lest there be some doubters among the readers of this paper, I have allowed my friend, the editor of this esteemed journal, which is to publish this story exclusively on Sunday next, free access to my archives, and he has selected as exhibits of evidence, to which I earnestly call your attention, the originals of the cuts which illustrate this chapter - viz:

I. A full-length portrait of Eve as she appeared at our first meeting.

II. Portraits of Cain and Abel at the ages of two, five,

and seven.

III. The original plans and specifications of the Ark.

IV. Facsimile of her commission.

V. Portrait-sketch of myself and the false Noah, made at the time, and showing how difficult it would have been for any member of my family, save myself, to tell us apart.

VI. A cathode-ray photograph of the whale, showing myself, the original Jonah, seated inside.

VII. Facsimiles of the Shakespeare autographs, proving that he knew neither how to write nor to spell, and so of course proving effectually that I was not the author of his works.

It must be confessed that I read this article of Munchausen's with amazement, and I awaited with much excited curiosity the coming again of the manipulator of my type-writing machine. Surely a revelation of this nature should create a sensation in Hades, and I was anxious to learn how it was received. Boswell did not materialize, however, and for five nights I fairly raged with the fever of curiosity, but on the sixth night the familiar tinkle of the bell announced an arrival, and I flew to the machine and breathlessly cried:

"Hullo, old chap, how did it come out?"

The reply was as great a surprise as I have yet had, for it was not Boswell, Jim Boswell, who answered my question.

IV

A CHAT WITH XANTHIPPE

The machine stopped its clicking the moment I spoke, and the words, "Hullo, old chap!" were no sooner uttered than my face grew red as a carnation pink. I felt as if I had committed some dreadful faux-pas, and instead of gazing steadfastly into the vacant chair, as I had been wont to do in my conversation with Boswell, my eyes fell, as though the invisible occupant of the chair were regarding me with a look of indignant scorn.

"I beg your pardon," I said.

"I should think you might," returned the types. "Hullo, old chap!" is no way to address a woman you've never had the honor of meeting, even if she is of the most advanced sort. No amount of newness in a woman gives a man the right to be disrespectful to her."

"I didn't know," I explained. "Really, miss, I -"

"Madame," interrupted the machine, "not miss. I am a married woman, sir, which makes of your rudeness an even more reprehensible act. It is well enough to affect a good-fellowship with young unmarried females, but when you attempt to be flippant with a married woman -"

"But I didn't know, I tell you," I appealed. "How should I? I supposed it was Boswell I was talking to, and he and I have become very good friends."

"Humph!" said the machine. "You're a chum of Boswell's, eh?"

"Well, not exactly a chum, but - " I began.

"But you go with him?" interrupted the lady.

"To an extent, yes," I confessed.

"And does he GO with you?" was the query. "If he does, permit me to depart at once. I should not feel quite in my element in a house where the editor of a Sunday newspaper was an attractive guest. If you like that sort of thing, your tastes -"

"I do not, madame," I replied, quickly. "I prefer the opium habit to the Sunday-newspaper habit, and if I thought Boswell was merely a purveyor of what is known as Sunday literature, which depends on the goodness of the day to offset its shortcomings, I should forbid him the house."

A distinct sigh of relief emanated from the chair.

"Then I may remain," was the remark rapidly clicked off on the machine.

"I am glad," said I. "And may I ask whom I have the honor of addressing?"

"Certainly," was the immediate response. "My name is Socrates, nee Xanthippe."

I instinctively cowered. Candidly, I was afraid. Never in my life before had I met a woman whom I feared. Never in my life have I wavered in the presence of the sex which cheers, but I have always felt that while I could hold my own with Elizabeth, withstand the wiles of Cleopatra, and manage the recalcitrant Katherine even as did Petruchio, Xanthippe was another story altogether, and I wished I had gone to the club. My first impulse was to call up-stairs to my wife and have her come down. She knows how to handle the new woman far better than I do. She has never wanted to vote, and my collars are safe in her hands. She has frequently observed that while she had many things to be thankful for, her greatest blessing was that she was born a woman and not a man, and the new women of her native town never leave her presence without wondering in their own minds whether or not they are mere humorous contributions of the Almighty to a too serious world. I pulled myself together as best I could, and feeling that my better-half would perhaps decline the proffered invitation to meet with one of the most illustrious of her sex, I decided to fight my own battle. So I merely said:

"Really? How delightful! I have always felt that I should like to meet you, and here is one of my devoutest wishes gratified."

I felt cheap after the remark, for Mrs. Socrates, nee Xanthippe, covered five sheets of paper with laughter, with an occasional bracketing of the word "derisively," such as we find in the daily newspapers interspersed throughout the after-dinner speeches of a candidate of another party. Finally, to my relief, the oft-repeated "Ha-ha-ha!" ceased, and the line, "I never should have guessed it," closed her immediate contribution to our interchange of ideas.

"May I ask why you laugh?" I observed, when she had at length finished.

"Certainly," she replied. "Far be it from me to dispute the right of a man to ask any question he sees fit to ask. Is he not the lord of creation? Is not woman his abject slave? I not the whole difference between them purely economic? Is it not the law of supply and demand that rules them both, he by nature demanding and she supplying?"

Dear reader, did you ever encounter a machine, man-made, merely a mechanism of ivory, iron, and ink, that could sniff contemptuously? I never did before this encounter, but the infernal power of either this type-writer or this woman who manipulated its keys imparted to the atmosphere I was breathing a sniffing contemp-tuousness which I have never experienced anywhere outside of a London hotel, and then only when I ventured, as few Americans have dared, to complain of the ducal personage who presided over the dining-room, but who, I must confess, was conquered subsequently by a tip of ten shillings.

At any rate, there was a sniff of contempt imparted, as I have said, to the atmosphere I was breathing as Xanthippe answered my question, and the sniff saved me, just as it did in the London hotel, when I complained of the lordly lack of manners on the part of the head waiter. I asserted my independence.

"Don't trouble yourself," I put in. "Of course I shall be interested in anything you may choose to say, but as a gentleman I do not care to put a woman to any incon-venience and I do not press the question."

And then I tried to crush her by adding, "What a lovely day we have had," as if any subject other than the most commonplace was not demanded by the situation.

"If you contemplate discussing the weather," was the retort, "I wish you would kindly seek out some one else with whom to do it. I am not one of your latter-day sit-out-on-the-stairs-while-the-others-dance girls. I am, as I have always been, an ardent admirer of principles, of great problems. For small talk I have no use."

"Very well, madame -" I began.

"You asked me a moment ago why I laughed," clicked the machine.

"I know it," said I. "But I withdraw the question. There is no great principle involved in a woman's laughter. I have known women who have laughed at a broken heart, as well as at jokes, which shows that there is no principle involved there; and as a problem, I have never cared enough about why women laugh to inquire deeply into it. If she'll just consent to laugh, I'm satisfied without inquiring into the causes thereof. Let us get down to an agreeable basis for yourself. What problem do you wish to discuss? Servants, baby-food, floor-polish, or the number of godets proper to the skirt of a well-dressed woman?"

I was regaining confidence in myself, and as I talked I ceased to fear her. Thought I to myself, "This attitude of supreme patronage is man's safest weapon against a woman. Keep cool, assume that there is no doubt of your superiority, and that she knows it. Appear to patronize her, and her own indignation will defeat her ends." It is a good principle generally. Among mortal women I have never known it to fail, and when I find myself worsted in an argument with one of man's greatest blessings, I always fall back upon it and am saved the ignominy of defeat. But this time I counted without my antagonist.

"Will you repeat that list of problems?" she asked, coldly.

"Servants, baby-food, floor-polish, and godets," I repeated, somewhat sheepishly, she took it so coolly.

"Very well," said Xanthippe, with a note of amusement in her manipulation of the keys. "If those are your subjects, let us discuss them. I am surprised to find an able-bodied man like yourself bothering with such problems, but I'll help you out of your difficulties if I can. No needy man shall ever say that I ignored his cry for help. What do you want to know about baby-food?"

This turning of the tables nonplussed me, and I didn't really know what to say, and so wisely said nothing, and the machine grew sharp in its clicking.

"You men!" it cried. "You don't know how fearfully shallow you are. I can see through you in a minute."

"Well," I said, modestly, "I suppose you can." Then calling my feeble wit to my rescue, I added, "It's only natural, since I've made a spectacle of myself."

"Not you!" cried Xanthippe. "You haven't even made a monocle of yourself."

And here we both laughed, and the ice was broken.

"What has become of Boswell?" I asked.

"He's been sent to the ovens for ten days for libelling Shakespeare and Adam and Noah and old Jonah," replied Xanthippe. "He printed an article alleged to have been written by Baron Munchausen, in which those four gentlemen were held up to ridicule and libelled grossly."

"And Munchausen?" I cried.

"Oh, the Baron got out of it by confessing that he wrote the article," replied the lady. "And as he swore to his confession the jury were convinced he was telling another one of his lies and acquitted him, so Boswell was sent up alone. That's why I am here. There isn't a man in all Hades that dared take charge of Boswell's paper - they're all so deadly afraid of the government, so I stepped in, and while Boswell is baking I'm attending to his editorial duties."

"But you spoke contemptuously of the Sunday newspapers awhile ago, Mrs. Socrates," said I.

"I know that," said Xanthippe, "but I've fixed that. I get out the Sunday edition on Saturdays."

"Oh - I see. And you like it?" I queried.

"First rate," she replied. "I'm in love with the work. I almost wish poor old Bos had been sentenced for ten years. I have enough of the woman in me to love minding other people's business, and, as far as I can find out, that's about all journalism amounts to. Sewing societies aren't to be mentioned in the same day with a newspaper for scandal and gossip, and, besides, I'm an ardent advocate of men's rights - have been for centuries - and I've got my first chance now to promulgate a few of my ideas. I'm really a man in all my views of life - that's the inevitable end of an advanced woman who persists in following her 'newness' to its logical conclusion. Her habits of thought gradually come to be those of a man. Even I have a great deal more sympathy with Socrates than I used to have. I used to think I was the one that should be emancipated, but I'm really reaching that stage in my manhood where I begin to believe that he needs emancipation."

"Then you admit, do you," I cried, with great glee, "that this new-woman business is all Tommy-rot?"

"Not by a great deal," snapped the machine. "Far from it. It's the salvation of the happy life. It is perfectly logical to say that the more manny a woman becomes, the more she is likely to sympathize with the troubles and trials which beset men."

I scratched my head and pulled the lobe of my ear in the hope of loosening an argument to confront her with, not that I disagreed with her entirely, but because I instinctively desired to oppose her as pleasantly disagreeably as I could. But the result was nil.

"I'm afraid you are right," I said.

"You're a truthful man," clicked the machine, laughingly. "You are afraid I'm right. And why are you afraid? Because you are one of those men who take a cynical view of woman. You want woman to be a mere lump of sugar, content to be left in a bowl until it pleases you in your high-and-mightiness to take her in the tongs and drop her into the coffee of your existence, to sweeten what would otherwise not please your taste - and like most men you prefer two or three lumps to one."

I could only cough. The lady was more or less right. I am very fond of sugar, though one lump is my allowance, and I never exceed it, whatever the temptation. Xanthippe continued.

"You criticise her because she doesn't understand you and your needs, forgetting that out of twenty-four hours of your daily existence your wife enjoys personally about twelve hours of your society, during eight of which you are lying flat on your back, snoring as though your life depended on it; but when she asks to be allowed to share your responsibilities as well as what, in her poor little soul, she thinks are your joys, you flare up and call her 'new' and 'advanced,' as if advancement were a crime. You ride off on your wheel for forty miles on your days of rest, and she is glad to have you do it, but when she wants a bicycle to ride, you think it's all wrong, immoral, and conducive to a weak heart. Bah!"

"I - ah -" I began.

"Yes you do," she interrupted. "You ah and you hem and you haw, but in the end you're a poor miserable social mugwump, conscious of your own magnificence and virtue, but nobody else ever can attain to your lofty plane. Now what I want to see among women is more good fellows. Suppose you regarded your wife as good a fellow as you think your friend Jones. Do you think you'd be running off to the club every night to play billiards with Jones, leaving your wife to enjoy her own society?"

"Perhaps not," I replied, "but that's just the point. My wife isn't a good fellow."

"Exactly, and for that reason you seek out Jones. You

have a right to the companionship of the good fellow - that's what I'm going to advocate. I've advanced far enough to see that on the average in the present state of woman she is not a suitable companion for man - she has none of the qualities of a chum to which he is entitled. I'm not so blind but that I can see the faults of my own sex, particularly now that I have become so very masculine myself. Both sexes should have their rights, and that is the great policy I'm going to hammer at as long as I have Boswell's paper in charge. I wish you might see my editorial page for to-morrow; it is simply fine. I urge upon woman the necessity of joining in with her husband in all his pleasures whether she enjoys them or not. When he lights a cigar, let her do the same; when he calls for a cocktail, let her call for another. In time she will begin to understand him. He understands her pleasures, and often he joins in with them - opera, dances, lectures; she ought to do the same, and join in with him in his pleasures, and after a while they'll get upon a common basis, have their clubs together, and when that happy time comes, when either one goes out the other will also go, and their companionship will be perfect."

"But you objected to my calling you old chap when we first met," said I. "Is that quite consistent?"

"Of course," retorted the lady. "We had never met before, and, besides, doctors do not always take their own medicine."

"But that women ought to become good fellows is what you're going to advocate, eh?" said I.

"Yes," replied Xanthippe. "It's excellent, don't you think?"

"Superb," I answered, "for Hades. It's just my idea of how things ought to be in Hades. I think, however, that we mortals will stick to the old plan for a little while yet; most of us prefer to marry wives rather than old chaps."

The remark seemed so to affect my visitor that I suddenly became conscious of a sense of loneliness.

"I don't wish to offend you," I said, "but I rather like to keep the two separate. Aren't you man enough yet to see the value of variety?"

But there was no answer. The lady had gone. It was evident that she considered me unworthy of further attention.

V

THE EDITING OF XANTHIPPE

After my interview with Xanthippe, I hesitated to approach the type-writer for a week or two. It did a great deal of clicking after the midnight hour had struck, and I was consumed with curiosity to know what was going on, but I did not wish to meet Mrs. Socrates again, so I held aloof until Boswell should have served his sentence. I was no longer afraid of the woman, but I do fear the good fellow of the weaker sex, and I deemed it just as well to keep out of any and all disputes that might arise from a casual conversation with a creature of that sort. An agreement with a real good fellow, even when it ends in a row, is more or less diverting; but a disputation with a female good fellow places a man at a disadvantage. The argumentum ad hominem is not an easy thing with men, but with women it is impossible. Hence, I let the type-writer click and ring for a fortnight.

Finally, to my relief, I recognized Boswell's touch upon the keys and sauntered up to the side of the machine.

"Is this Boswell - Jim Boswell?" I inquired.

"All that's left of him," was the answer. "How have you been?"

"Very well," said I. And then it seemed to me that tact required that I should not seem to know that he had been in the superheated jail of the Stygian country. So I observed, "You've been off on a vacation, eh?"

"How do you know that?" was the immediate response.

"Well," I put in, "you've been absent for a fortnight, and you look more or less - ah - burned."

"Yes, I am," replied the deceitful editor. "Very much burned, in fact. I've been - er - I've been playing golf with a friend down in Cimmeria."

"I envy you," I observed, with an inward chuckle.

"You wouldn't if you knew the links," replied Boswell, sadly. "They're awfully hard. I don't know any harder course than the Cimmerian."

And then I became conscious of a mistrustful gaze fastened upon me.

"See here," clicked the machine. "I thought I was invisible to you? If so, how do you know I look burned?"

I was cornered, and there was only one way out of it, and that was by telling the truth. "Well, you are invisible, old chap," I said. "The fact is, I've been told of your trouble, and I know what you have undergone."

"And who told you?" queried Boswell.

"Your successor on the Gazette, Madame Socrates, nee Xanthippe," I replied.

John Kendrick Bangs

"Oh, that woman - that woman!" moaned Boswell, through the medium of the keys. "Has she been here, using this machine too? Why didn't you stop her before she ruined me completely?"

"Ruined you?" I cried.

"Well, next thing to it," replied Boswell. "She's run my paper so far into the ground that it will take an almighty powerful grip to pull it out again. Why, my dear boy, when I went to - to the ovens, I had a circulation of a million, and when I came back that woman had brought it down to eight copies, seven of which have already been returned. All in ten days, too."

"How do you account for it?" I asked.

"'Side Talks with Men' helped, and 'The Man's Corner' did a little, but the editorial page did the most of it. It was given over wholly to the advancement of certain Xanthippian ideas, which were very offensive to my women readers, and which found no favor among the men. She wants to change the whole social structure. She thinks men and women are the same kind of animal, and that both need to be educated on precisely the same lines - the girls to be taught business, the boys to go through a course of domestic training. She called for subscriptions for a cooking-school for boys, and demanded the endowment of a commercial college for girls, and wound up by insisting upon a uniform dress for both sexes. I tell you, if you'd worked for years to establish a dignified newspaper the way I have, it would have broken your heart to see the suggested fashion-plates that woman printed. The uniform dress was a holy terror. It was a combination of all the worst features of modern garb. Trousers were to be universal and compulsory; sensible masculine coats were discarded entirely, and puffed-sleeved dress-coats were substituted. Stiff collars were abolished in favor of ribbons, and rosettes cropped up everywhere. Imagine it if you can - and everybody in all Hades was to be forced into garments of that sort!"

"I should enjoy seeing it," I said.

"Possibly - but you wouldn't enjoy wearing it," retorted the machine. "And then that woman's funny column - it was frightful. You never saw such jokes in your life; every one of them contained a covert attack upon man. There was only one good thing in it, and that was a bit of verse called 'Fair Play for the Little Girls.' It went like this:

> "'If little boys, when they are young,
> Can go about in skirts,
> And wear upon their little backs
> Small broidered girlish shirts,
> Pray why cannot the little girls,
> When infants, have a chance
> To toddle on their little ways
> In little pairs of pants?'"

"That isn't at all bad," said I, smiling in spite of poor Boswell's woe. "If the rest of the paper was on a par with that I don't see why the circulation fell off."

"Well, she took liberties, that's all," said Boswell. "For instance, in her 'Side Talks with Men' she had something like this: 'Napoleon - It is rather difficult to say just what you can do with your last season's cocked-hat. If you were to purchase five yards of one-inch blue ribbon, cut it into three strips of equal length, and fasten one end to each of the three corners of the hat, tying the other ends into a choux, it would make a very acceptable work-basket to send to your grandmother at Christmas.' Now Napoleon never asked that woman for advice on the subject. Then there was an answer to a purely fictitious inquiry from Solomon which read: 'It all depends on local custom. In Salt Lake City, and in London at the time of Henry the Eighth, it was not considered necessary to be off with the old love before being on with the new, but latterly the growth of monopolistic ideas tends towards the uniform rate of one at a time.' A purely gratuitous fling, that was, at one of my most eminent patrons, or rather two of them, for latterly both Solomon and Henry the Eighth have yielded to the tendency of the times and gone into business, which they have paid me well to advertise. Solomon has established an 'Information Bureau,' where advice can always be had from the 'Wise-man,' as he calls himself, on payment of a small fee; while Henry, taking advantage of his superior equipment over any English king that ever lived, has founded and liberally advertised his 'Chaperon Company (Limited).' It's a great thing even in Hades for young people to be chaperoned by an English queen, and Henry has been smart enough to see it, and having seven or eight queens, all in good standing, he has been doing a great business. Just look at it from a business point of view. There are seven nights in every week, and something going on somewhere all the time, and queens in demand. With a queen quoted so low as $100 a night, Henry can make nearly $5000 a week, or $260,000 a year, out of evening chaperonage alone; and when, in addition to this, yachting-parties up the Styx and slumming-parties throughout the country are being constantly given, the man's opportunity to make half a million a year is in plain sight. I'm told that he netted over $500,000 last year; and of course he had to advertise to get it, and this Xanthippe woman goes out of her way to get in a nasty little fling at one of my mainstays for his matrimonial propensities."

"Failing utterly to see," said I, "that, in marrying so many times, Henry really paid a compliment to her sex which is without parallel in royal circles."

"Well, nearly so," said Boswell. "There have been other kings who were quite as complimentary to the ladies, but Henry was the only man among them who insisted on marrying them all."

"True," said I. "Henry was eminently proper - but then he had to be."

"Yes," said Boswell, with a meditative tap on the letter Y. "Yes - he had to be. He was the head of the Church, you know."

"I know it," I put in. "I've always had a great deal of sympathy for Henry. He has been very much misjudged by posterity. He was the father of the really first new woman, Elizabeth, and his other daughter, Mary, was such a vindictive person."

"You are a very fair man, for an American," said Boswell. "Not only fair, but rare. You think about things."

"I try to," said I, modestly. "And I've really thought a great deal about Henry, and I've truly seen a valid reason for his continuous matrimonial performances. He set himself up against the Pope, and he had to be consistent in his antagonism."

"He did, indeed," said Boswell. "A religious discussion is a hard one."

"And Henry was consistent in his opposition," said I. "He didn't yield a jot on any point, and while a great many people criticise him on the score of his wives – particularly on their number - I feel that I have in very truth discovered his principle."

"Which was?" queried Boswell.

"That the Pope was wrong in all things," said I.

"So he said," commented Boswell.

"And being wrong in all things, celibacy was wrong," said I.

"Exactly," ejaculated Boswell.

"Well, then," said I, "if celibacy is wrong, the surest way to protest against it is to marry as many times as you can."

"By Jove!" said Boswell, tapping the keys yearningly, as though he wished he might spare his hand to shake mine, "you are a man after my own heart."

"Thanks, old chap," said I, reaching out my hand and shaking it in the air with my visionary friend - "thanks. I've studied these things with some care, and I've tried to find a reason for everything in life as I know it. I have always regarded Henry as a moral man - as is natural, since in spite of all you can say he is the real head of the English Church. He wasn't willing to be married a second or a seventh time unless he was really a widower. He wasn't as long in taking notice again as some modern widowers that I have met, but I do not criticise him on that score. I merely attribute his record to his kingly nature, which involves necessarily a quickness of decision and a decided perception of the necessities which is sadly lacking in people who are born to a lesser station in life. England demanded a queen, and he invariably met the demand, which shows that he knew something of political economy as well as of matrimony; and as I see it, being an American, a man needs to know something of political economy to be a good ruler. So many of our statesmen have acquired a merely kindergarten knowledge of the science, that we have had many object-lessons of the disadvantages of a merely elementary knowledge of the subject. To come right down to it, I am a great admirer of Henry. At any rate, he had the courage of his heart-convictions."

"You really surprise me," tapped Boswell. "I never expected to find an American so thoroughly in sympathy with kings and their needs."

"Oh, as for that," said I, "in America we are all kings and we are not without our needs, matrimonial and otherwise, only our courts are not quite so expeditious as Henry's little axe. But what was Henry's attitude towards this extraordinary flight of Xanthippe's?"

"Wrath," said Boswell. "He was very much enraged, and withdrew his advertisements, declined to give our society reporters the usual accounts of the functions his wives chaperoned, and, worst of all, has withdrawn himself and induced others to withdraw from the symposium I was preparing for my special Summer Girls' issue, which is to appear in August, on 'How Men Propose.' He and Brigham Young and Solomon and Bonaparte had agreed to dictate graphic accounts of how they had done it on various occasions, and Queen Elizabeth, who probably had more proposals to the square minute that any other woman on record, was to write the introduction. This little plan, which was really the idea of genius, is entirely shattered by Mrs. Socrates's infernal interference."

"Nonsense," said I. "Don't despair. Why don't you come out with a plain statement of the facts? Apologize."

"You forget, my dear sir," interposed Boswell, "that one of the fundamental principles of Hades as an institution is that excuses don't count. It isn't a place for repentance so much as for expiation, and I might apologize nine times a minute for forty years and would still have to suffer the penalty of the offence. No, there is nothing to be done but to begin my newspaper work again, build up again the institution that Xanthippe has destroyed, and bear my misfortunes like a true spirit."

"Spoken like a philosopher!" I cried. "And if I can help you, my dear Boswell, count upon me. In anything you may do, whether you start a monthly magazine, a sporting weekly, or a purely American Sunday new-spaper, you are welcome to anything I can do for you."

"You are very kind," returned Boswell, appreciatively, "and if I need your services I shall be glad to avail myself of them. Just at present, however, my plans are so fully prepared that I do not think I shall have to call upon you. With Sherlock Holmes engaged to write twelve new detective stories; Poe to look after my tales of horror; D'Artagnan dictating his personal memoirs; Lucretia Borgia running my Girls' Department; and others too numerous to mention, I have a sufficient supply of stuff to fill up; but if you feel like writing a few poems for me I may be able to use them as fillers, and they may help to make your name so well known in Hades that next year I shall be able to print a Worldly Letter from you every week with a good chance of its proving popular."

And with this promise Boswell left me to get out the first number of The Cimmerian: a Sunday Magazine for all. Taking him at his word, I sent him the following poem a few days later:

LOCALITY

Whither do we drift,
Insensate souls, whose every breath
Foretells the doom of nothingness?
Yet onward, upward let it be
Through all the myriad circles
Of the ensuing years -
And then, pray what?
Alas! 'tis all, and never shall be stated.
Atoms, yet atomless we drift,
But whitherward?

I had intended this for one of our leading magazines, but it seemed so to lack the mystical quality, which is essential to a successful magazine poem in our sphere, that I deemed it best to try it on Boswell.

VI

THE BOSWELL TOURS:
PERSONALLY CONDUCTED

It was and will no doubt be considered, even by those who are not too friendly towards myself, a daring idea, and it was all my own. One night, several weeks after the interview with Boswell just narrated, the idea came to me simultaneously with the first tapping of the keys for the evening upon the Enchanted Type-Writer. It was Boswell's touch that summoned me from my divan. My family were on the eve of departure for a month's rest from care and play in the mountains, and I was looking forward to a period of very great loneliness. But as Boswell materialized and began his work upon the machine, the great idea flashed across my mind, and I resolved to "play it" for all it was worth.

"Jim," said I, as I approached the vacant chair in which he sat - for by this time the great biographer and I had got upon terms of familiarity - "Jim," said I, "I've got a very gloomy prospect ahead of me."

"Well, why not?" he tapped off. "Where do you expect to have your gloomy prospects? They can't very well be behind you."

"Humph!" said I. "You are facetious this evening."

"Not at all," he replied. "I have been spending the day with my old-time boss, Samuel Johnson, and I am so saturated with purism that I hardly know where I am. From the Johnsonian point of view you have expressed yourself ill -"

"Well, I am ill," I retorted. "I don't know how far you are acquainted with home life, but I do know that there is no greater homesickness in the world than that of the man who is sick of home."

"I am not an imitator," said Boswell, "but I must imitate you to the extent of saying humph! I quote you, and, doing so, I honor you. But really, I never thought you could be sick of home, as you put it - you who are so happy at home and who so wildly hate being away from home."

"I'm not surprised at that, my dear Boswell," said I. "But you are, of course, familiar with the phrase 'Stone walls do not a prison make?'"

"I've heard it," said Boswell.

"Well, there's another equally valid phrase which I have not yet heard expressed by another, and it is this: 'Stone walls do not a home make.'"

"It isn't very musical, is it?" said he.

"Not very," I answered, "but we don't all live magazine lives, do we? We have occasionally a sentiment, a feeling, out of which we do not try 'to make copy.' It is undoubtedly a truth which I have not yet seen voiced by any modern poet of my acquaintance, not even by the dead-baby poets, that home is not always preferable to

John Kendrick Bangs

some other things. At any rate, it is my feeling, and is shortly to represent my condition. My home, you know. It has its walls and its pictures, and its thousand and one comforts, and its associations, but when my wife and my children are away, and the four walls do not re-echo the voices of the children, and my library lacks the presence of madame, it ceases truly to be home, and if I've got to stay here during the month of August alone I must have diversion, else I shall find myself as badly off as the butterfly man, to whom a vaudeville exhibition is the greatest joy in life."

"I think you are queer," said Boswell.

"Well, I am not," said I. "However low we may set the standard of man, Mr. B." - and I called him Mr. B. instead of Jim, because I wished to be severe and yet retain the basis of familiarity - "however low we may set the standard of man, I think man as a rule prefers his home to the most seductive roof-garden life in existence."

"Wherefore?" said he, coldly.

"Wherefore my home about to become unattractive through the absence of my boys and their mother, I shall need some extraordinary diversion to accomplish my happiness. Now if you can come here, why can't others? Suppose to-night you dash off on the machine a lot of invitations to the pleasantest people in Hades to come up here with you and have an evening on earth, which isn't all bad."

"It's a scheme and a half," said Boswell, with more enthusiasm than I had expected. "I'll do it, only instead of trying to get these people to make a pilgrimage to your shrine, which I think they would decline to do - Shakespeare, for instance, wouldn't give a tuppence to inspect your birthplace as you have inspected his - I'll institute a series of 'Boswell's Personally Conducted Pleasure Parties,' and make you my agent here. That, you see, will naturally make your home our headquarters, and I think the scheme would work a charm, because there are a great many well-known Stygians who are curious to revisit the scenes of their earlier state, but who are timid about coming on their own responsibility."

"I see," said I. "Immortals are but mortal after all, with all the timidity and weaknesses of mortality. But I agree to the proposition, and if you wish it I'll prepare to give them a rousing old time."

"And be sure to show them something characteristic," said Boswell.

"I will," I replied; "I may even get up a trolley-party for them."

"I don't know what a trolley-party is, but it sounds well," said Boswell, "and I'll advertise the enterprise at once. 'Boswell's Personally Conducted Pleasure Parties. First Series, No. 1. Trolleying Through Hoboken. For the Round Trip, Four Dollars. Supper and All Expenses Included. No Tips. Extra Lady's Ticket, One Dollar.'"

"Hold on!" I cried. "That can't be. These affairs will really have to be stag-parties - with my wife away, you know."

"Not if we secure a suitable chaperon," said Boswell.

"Anyhow!" said I, with great positiveness. "You don't

suppose that in the absence of my family I'm going to have my neighbors see me cavorting about the country on a trolley-car full of queens and duchesses and other females of all ages? Not a bit of it, my dear James. I'm not a strictly conventional person, but there are some points between which I draw lines. I've got to live on this earth for a little while yet, and until I leave it I must be guided more or less in what I do by what the world approves or disapproves."

"Very well," Boswell answered. "I suppose you are right, but in the autumn, when your family has returned -"

"We can discuss the matter again," said I, resolved to put off the question for as long a time as I could, for I candidly confess that I had no wish to make myself responsible for the welfare of such Stygian ladies as might avail themselves of the opportunity to go off on one of Boswell's tours. "Show the value and beauties of your plan to the influential men of Hades first, my dear Boswell," I added, "and then if they choose they can come again and bring their wives with them on their own responsibility."

"I fancy that is the best plan, but we ought to have some variety in these tours," he replied. "A trolley-party, however successful, would not make a great season for an entertainment bureau, would it?"

"No, indeed," said I. "You are perfectly right about that. What you want is one function a week during the summer season. Open with the trolley-party as No. 1 of your first series. Follow this with 'An Evening of Vaudeville: The Grand Tour of the Roof Gardens.' After that have a 'Sunday at the Sea-side - Surf Bathing, Summer Girls and Sand.' That would make a mighty attractive line for your advertisement."

"Magnificent. I don't see why you don't give up poetry and magazine work and get a position as poster-writer for a circus. You are only a mediocre magazinist, but in the poster business you'd be a genius."

This was tapped off with such manifest sincerity that I could not take offence, so I thanked him and resumed.

"The grand finale of your first series might be 'A Tandem Scorch: A Century Run on a Bicycle Built for Two Hundred!'"

"Magnificent!" cried Boswell, with such enthusiasm that I feared he would smash the machine. "I'll devote a whole page of my Sunday issue to the prospectus - but, to return to the woman question, we ought really to have something to announce for them. Hades hath no fury like a woman scorned, and I can't afford to scorn the sex. You needn't have anything to do with them if you don't want to - only tell me something I can announce, and I'll make Henry the Eighth solid again by putting that branch of the enterprise in his wives' hands. In that way I'll kill two birds with one stone."

"That's all very well, Boswell, but I'm afraid I can't," said I. "It's hard enough to know how to please a mortal woman without attempting to get up a series of picnics for the rather miscellaneous assortment of ladies who form your social structure below. All men are alike, and man's pleasures in all times have been generally the same, but every woman is unique. I never knew two who were alike, and if it's all the same to you I'd rather you left me out of your ladies' tours altogether. Of course I know that even the Queen of Sheba would enjoy a visit to a

Monday sale at one of our big department stores, and I am quite as well aware that nine out of ten women in Hades or out of it would enjoy the millinery exhibition at the opera matinee - and if these two ideas impress you at all you are welcome to them - but beyond this I have nothing to suggest."

"Well, I'm sure those two ideas are worth a great deal," returned Boswell, making a note of them; "I shall announce four trips to Monday sales -"

"Call 'em 'To Bargaindale and Back: The Great Marked-down Tour,' and be sure you add, 'For Able-bodied Women Only. No Tickets Issued Except on Recommendation of your Family Physician.' This is especially important, for next to a war or a football match there's nothing that I know of that is quite so dangerous to the participants as a bargain day."

"I'll bear what you say in mind," quoth Boswell, and he made a note of my injunction. "And immediately upon my return to Hades I will request an audience with Henry's queens, and ask them to devise a number of other tours likely to prove profitable and popular."

Shortly after my visitor departed and I retired. The next day my family deserted me and went to the mountains, and all my fears as to the inordinate sense of loneliness which was to be my lot were realized. Even Boswell neglected me apparently for a week. I went to my desk daily and returned at night hoping that my type-writer would bring forth something of an interesting nature, but naught other than disappointment awaited me. For a whole blessed week I was thrown back upon the society of my neighbors for diversion. The type-writer gave no sign of being.

Little did I guess that Boswell was busy working up my scheme in his Stygian home!

But it came to pass finally that I was roused up. Walking one morning to my desk to find a bit of memoranda I needed, I discovered a type-written slip marked, "No time for small talk. Boswell's tours grand success. Trolley-party to-night. Ten cars wanted. Jim."

It was a large order for a town like mine, where forty thousand people have to get along with five cars - two open ones for winter and two closed for summer, and one, which we have never seen, which is kept for use in the repair-shop. I was in despair. Ten car-loads of immortals coming to my house for a trolley-party under such conditions! It was frightful! I did the best I could, however.

I ordered one trolley-car to be ready at eight, and a large variety of good things edible and drinkable, the latter to be held subject to the demand-notes of our guests.

As may be imagined, I did little real work that day, and when I returned home at night I was on tenter-hooks lest something should go wrong; but fortunately Boswell himself came early and relieved me of my worry - in fact, he was at the machine when I entered the house.

"Well," he said, "have you the ten cars?"

"What do you take me for," said I, "a trolley-car trust? Of course I haven't. There are only five cars in town, one of which is kept in the repair-shop for effect. I've hired one."

"Humph!" he cried. "What will the kings do?"

"Kings!" I cried. "What kings?"

"I have nine kings and one car-load of common souls besides for this affair," he explained. "Each king wants a special car."

"Kings be jiggered!" said I. "A trolley-party, my much beloved James, is an essentially democratic institution, and private cars are not de rigueur. If your kings choose to come, let 'em hang on by the straps."

"But I've charged 'em extra!" cried Boswell.

"That's all right," said I, "they receive extra. They have the ride plus the straps, with the privilege of standing out on the platform and ringing the gong if they want to. The great thing about the trolley-party is that there's no private car business about it."

"Well, I don't know," Boswell murmured, reflectively. "If Charles the First and Louis Fourteenth don't kick about being crowded in with all the rest, I can stand anything that Frederick the Great or Nero might say; but those two fellows are great sticklers for the royal prerogative."

"There isn't any such thing as royal prerogative on a trolley-car," I retorted, "and if they don't like what they get they can sit down in the waiting-room and wait until we get back."

But Boswell's fears were not realized. Charles and Louis were perfectly delighted with the trolley-party, and long before we reached home the former had rung up the fare-register to its full capacity, while the latter, a half-a-dozen times, delightedly occupied himself in mastering the intricacies of the overhead wire. The trolley-party was an undoubted success. The same remains to be said of the vaudeville expedition of the following week. The same guests and potentates attended this, to the number of twenty, and the Boswell tours were accounted a great enterprise, and bade fair to redeem the losses of the eminent journalist incurred during Xanthippe's administration of his affairs; but after the bicycle night I had to withdraw from the combination to save my reputation. The fact upon which I had not counted was that my neighbors began to think me insane. I had failed to remember that none of these visiting spirits was visible to us in this material world, and while my fellow-townsmen were disposed to lay up my hiring of a special trolley-car for my own private and particular use against the eccentricity of genius, they marvelled greatly that I should purchase twenty of the best seats at a vaudeville show seemingly for my own exclusive use. When, besides this, they saw me start off apparently alone on one tandem bicycle, followed by twenty-eight other empty wheels, which they could not know were manipulated by some of the most famous legs in the history of the world, from Noah's down to those of Henry Fielding the novelist, they began to regard me as something uncanny.

Nor can I blame them. It seems to me that if I saw one man scorching along a road alone on a tandem bicycle chatting to an empty front-seat, I should think him queer, but if following in his wake I perceived twenty-eight other wheels, scorching up hill and down dale without any visible motive power, I should regard him as one who was in league with the devil himself.

Nevertheless, I judge from what Boswell has told me that I am regarded in Hades as a great benefactor of the people there, for having established a series of excursions from that world into this, a service which has done much to convince the Stygians that after all, if only by contrast, the life below has its redeeming features.

VII

AN IMPORTANT DECISION

For some time after the organization of the Pleasure Tours, the Enchanted Type-Writer appeared to be deserted. Night after night I watched over it with great care lest I should lose any item of interest that might come to me from below, but, much to my sorrow, things in Hades appeared to be dull - so dull that the machine was not called into requisition at all. I little guessed what important matters were transpiring in that wonderful country. Had I done so, I doubt I should have waited so patiently, although my only method of getting there was suicide, for which diversion I have very little liking. On the twenty-fourth night of waiting, however, the welcome sound of the bell dragged me forth from my comfortable couch, whither, expecting nothing, I had retired early.

"Glad to hear your pleasant tinkle again," I said. "I've missed you."

"I'm glad to get back," returned Boswell, for it was he who was manipulating the keys. "I've been so infernally busy, however, over the court news, that I haven't had a minute to spare."

"Court news, eh?" I said. "You are going to open up a

society column, are you?"

"Not I," he replied. "It's the other kind of a court. We've been having some pretty hot litigation down in Hades since I was here last. The city of Cimmeria has been suing the State of Hades for ten years back dog-taxes."

"For what?" I cried.

"Unpaid dog-taxes for ten years," Boswell explained. "We have just as much government below in our cities as you have, and I will say for Hades that our cities are better run than yours."

"I suppose that is due to the fact that when a man gets to Hades he immediately becomes a reformer," I suggested, with a wink at the machine, which somehow or other did not seem to appreciate the joke.

"Possibly," observed Boswell. "Whatever the reason, however, the fact remains that Cimmeria is a well-governed city, and, what is more, it isn't afraid to assert its rights even as against old Apollyon himself."

"It's safe enough for a corporation," said I. "Much safer for a corporation which has no soul, than for an individual who has. You can't torture a city -"

"Oh, can't you!" laughed Boswell. "Humph. Apollyon can make it as hot for a city as he can for an individual. It is evident that you never heard of Sodom and Gomorrah - which is surprising to me, since your jokes about Lot's wife being too fresh and getting salted down, would seem to indicate that you had heard something about the punishment those cities underwent."

"You are right, Bozzy," I said. "I had forgotten. But tell me about the dog-tax. Does the State own a dog?"

"Does it?" roared Boswell. "Why, my dear fellow, where were you brought up and educated. Does the State own a dog!"

"That's what I asked you," I put in, meekly. "I may be very ignorant, unless you mean the kind that we have in our legislatures, called the watch-dogs of the treasury, or, perhaps, the dogs of war. But I never thought any city would be crazy enough to make the government take out a license for them."

"Never heard of a beast named Cerberus, I suppose?" said Boswell.

"Yes, I have," I answered. "He guards the gates to the infernal regions."

"Well - he's the bone of contention," said Boswell. "You see, about ten years ago the people of Cimmeria got rather tired of the condition of their streets. They were badly paved. They were full of good intentions, but the citizens thought they ought to have something more lasting, so they voted to appropriate an enormous sum for asphalting. They didn't realize how sloppy asphalt would become in that climate, but after the asphalt was put down they found out, and a Beelzebub of a time of it they had. Pegasus sprained his off hind leg by slipping on it, Bucephalus got into it with all four feet and had to be lifted out with a derrick, and every other fine horse we had was more or less injured, and the damage suits against the city were enormous. To remedy this, the asphalting was taken up and a Nicholson wood pavement was put down. This was worse than the other.

It used to catch fire every other night, and, finally, to protect their houses, the people rose up en masse and ripped it all to pieces.

"This necessitated a third new pavement, of Belgian blocks, to pay for which the already overburdened city of Cimmeria had to issue bonds to an enormous amount, all of which necessitated an increase of taxes. Naturally, one of the first taxes to be imposed was a dog-tax, and it was that which led to this lawsuit, which, I regret to say, the city has lost, although Judge Blackstone's decision was eminently fair."

"Wouldn't the State pay?" I asked.

"Yes - on Cerberus as one dog," said Boswell. "The city claimed, however, that Cerberus was more than that, and endeavored to collect on three dogs - one license for each head. This the State declined to pay, and out of this grew further complications of a distressing nature. The city sent its dog-catchers up to abscond with the dog, intending to cut off two of its heads, and return the balance as being as much of the beast as the State was entitled to maintain on a single license. It was an unfortunate move, for when Cerberus himself took the situation in, which he did at a glance, he nabbed the dog-catcher by the coat-tails with one pair of jaws, grabbed hold of his collar with another, and shook him as he would a rat, meanwhile chewing up other portions of the unfortunate official with his third set of teeth. The functionary was then carried home on a stretcher, and subsequently sued the city for damages, which he recovered.

"Another man was sent out to lure the ferocious beast to the pound with a lasso, but it worked no better than the previous attempt. The lasso fell all right tight about one of the animal's necks, but his other two heads immediately set to work and gnawed the rope through, and then set off after the dog-catcher, overtaking him at the very door of the pound. This time he didn't do any biting, but lifting the dog-catcher up with his various sets of teeth, fastened to his collar, coat-tails, and feet respectively, carried him yelling like a trooper to the end of the wharf and dropped him into the Styx. The result of this was nervous prostration for the dog-catcher, another suit for damages for the city, and a great laugh for the State authorities. In fact," Boswell added, confidentially, "I think perhaps the reason why the Prime-minister hasn't got Apollyon to hang the whole city government has been due to the fun they've got out of seeing Cerberus and the city fighting it out together. There's no doubt about it that he is a wonderful dog, and is quite capable of taking care of himself."

"But the outcome of the case?" I asked, much interested.

"Defeat for the city," said Boswell. "Failing to enforce its authority by means of its servants, the city undertook to recover by due process of law. The dog-catchers were powerless; the police declined to act on the advice of the commissioners, since dog-catching was not within their province; and the fire department averred that it was designed for the putting out of fires and not for extinguishing fiery canines like Cerberus. The dog, meanwhile, to show his contempt for the city, chewed the license-tag off the neck upon which it had been placed, and dropped it into a smelting-pot inside the gates of the infernal regions that was reserved to bring political prisoners to their senses, and, worse than all, made a perfect nuisance of himself by barking all day and baying all night, rain or shine."

"Papers in a suit at law were then served on Mazarin and the other members of Apollyon's council, the causes of complaint were recited, and damages for ten years back taxes on two dogs, plus the amounts recovered from the city by the two injured dog-catchers, were demanded. The suit was put upon the calendar, and Apollyon himself sat upon the bench with Judge Blackstone, before whom the case was to be tried.

"On both sides the arguments were exceedingly strong. Coke appeared for the city and Catiline for the State. After the complaint was read, the attorney for the State put in his answer, that the State's contention was that the ordinance had been complied with, that Cerberus was only one dog, and that the license had been paid; that the license having been paid, the dog-catchers had no right to endeavor to abduct the animal, and that having done so they did it at their own peril; that the suit ought to be dismissed, but that for the fun of it the State was perfectly willing to let it go on.

"In rebuttal the plaintiff claimed that Cerberus was three dogs to all intents and purposes, and the first dog-catcher was called to testify. After giving his name and address he was asked a few questions of minor importance, and then Coke asked:

"'Are you familiar with dogs?'

"'Moderately,' was the answer. 'I never got quite so intimate with one as I did with him.'

"'With whom?' asked Coke.

"'Cerberus,' replied the witness.

"'Do you consider him to be one dog, two dogs or three dogs?'

"'I object!' cried Catiline, springing to his feet. 'The question is a leading one.'

"'Sustained,' said Blackstone, with a nervous glance at Apollyon, who smiled reassuringly at him.

"'Ah, you say you know a dog when you see one?' asked Coke.

"'Yes,' said the witness, 'perfectly.'

"'Do you know two dogs when you see them, or even three?' asked Coke.

"'I do,' replied the witness.

"'And how many dogs did you see when you saw Cerberus?' asked Coke, triumphantly.

"'Three, anyhow,' replied the witness, with feeling, 'though afterwards I thought there was a whole bench-show atop of me.'

"'Your witness,' said Coke.

"A murmur of applause went through the court-room, at which Apollyon frowned; but his face cleared in a moment when Catiline rose up.

"'My cross-examination of this witness, your honor, will be confined to one question.' Then turning to the witness he said, blandly: 'My poor friend, if you considered Cerberus to be three dogs anyhow, why did you in your examination a moment since refer to the avalanche of caninity, of which you so affectingly speak, as him?'

"'He is a him,' said the witness.

"'But if there were three, should he not have been a them?'

"Coke swore profanely beneath his breath, and the witness squirmed about in his chair, confused and broken, while both Judge Blackstone and Apollyon smiled broadly. Manifestly the point of the defence had pierced the armor of the plaintiff.

"'Your witness for re-direct,' said Catiline.

"'No thanks,' retorted Coke; 'there are others,' and, motioning to his first witness to step down, he called the second dog-catcher.

"'What is your business?' asked Coke, after the usual preliminary questions.

"'I'm out of business. Livin' on my damages,' said the witness.

"'What damages?' asked Coke.

"'Them I got from the city for injuries did me by that there - I should say them there - dorgs, Cerberus.'

"'Them there what?' persisted Coke, to emphasize the point.

"'Dorgs,' said the witness, convincingly - 'D-o-r-g-s.'

"'Why s?' queried Coke. 'We may admit the r, but why the s?'

"'Because it's the pullural of dorg. Cerberus ain't any single-headed commission,' said the witness, who was something of a ward politician.

"'Why do you say that Cerberus is more than one dog?'

"'Because I've had experience,' replied the witness. 'I've seen the time when he was everywhere all at once; that's why I say he's more than one dorg. If he'd been only one dorg he couldn't have been anywhere else than where he was.'

"'When was that?'

"'When I lassoed him.'

"'Him?' remonstrated Coke.

"'Yes,' said the witness. 'I only caught one of him, and then the other two took a hand.'

"'Ah, the other two,' said Coke. 'You know dogs when you see them?'

"'I do, and he was all of 'em in a bunch,' replied the witness.

"'Your witness,' said Coke.

"'My friend,' said Catiline, rising quietly. 'How many men are you?'

"'One, sir,' was the answer.

"'Have you ever been in two places at once?'

"'Yes, sir.'

"'When was that?'

"'When I was in jail and in London all at the same time.'

"'Very good; but were you in two places on the day of this attack upon you by Cerberus?'

"'No, sir. I wish I had been. I'd have stayed in the other place.'

"'Then if you were in but one place yourself, how do you know that Cerberus was in more than one place?'

"'Well, I guess if you -'

"'Answer the question,' said Catiline.

"'Oh, well - of course -'

"'Of course,' echoed Catiline. 'That's it, your honor; it is only "of course," - and I rest my case. We have no witnesses to call. We have proven by their own witnesses that there is no evidence of Cerberus being more than one dog.'

"You ought to have heard the cheers as Catiline sat down," continued Boswell. "As for poor Coke, he was regularly knocked out, but he rose up to sum up his case as best he could. Blackstone, however, stopped him right at the beginning.

"'The counsel for the plaintiff might as well sit down,' he

said, 'and save his breath. I've decided this case in favor of the defendant long ago. It is plain to every one that Cerberus is only one dog, in spite of his many talents and manifest ability to be in several places at once, and inasmuch as the tax which is sued for is merely a dog-tax and not a poll-tax, I must render judgment for the defendants, with costs. Next case.'

"And the city of Cimmeria was thrown out of court," concluded Boswell. "Interesting, eh?"

"Very," said I. "But how will this affect Blackstone? Isn't he a City Judge?"

"No," replied Boswell; "he was, but his term expired this morning, and this afternoon Apollyon appointed him Chief Justice of the Supreme Court of Hades."

VIII

A HAND-BOOK TO HADES

"Boswell," said I, the other night, as the machine began to click nervously. "I have just received a letter from an unknown friend in Hawaii who wants to know how the prize-fight between Samson and Goliath came out that time when Kidd and his pirate crew stole the House-Boat on the Styx."

"Just wait a minute, please," the machine responded. "I am very busy just now mapping out the itinerary of the first series of the Boswell Personally Conducted Tours you suggested some time ago. I laid that whole proposition before the Entertainment Committee of the Associated Shades, and they have resolved unanimously to charter the Ex-Great Eastern from the Styx Navigation Company, and return to the scenes of their former glory, devoting a year to it."

"Going to take their wives?" I asked.

"I don't know," Boswell replied. "That is a matter outside of the jurisdiction of the committee and must be decided by a full vote of the club. I hope they will, however. As manager of the enterprise I need assistance, and there are some of the men who can't be managed by anybody except their wives, or mothers-in-law, anyhow.

I'll be through in a few minutes. Meanwhile let me hand you the latest product of the Boswell press."

With this the genial spirit produced from an invisible pocket a red-covered book bearing the delicious title of "Baedeker's Hades: A Hand-book for Travellers," which has entirely superseded, according to the advertisement on the fly-leaves, such books as Virgil and Dante's Inferno as the best guide to the lower regions, as well it might, for it appeared on perusal to have been prepared with as much care as one of the more material guide-books of the same publisher, which so greatly assist travellers on this side of the Stygian River.

Some time, if Boswell will permit, I shall endeavor to have this little volume published in this country since it contains many valuable hints to the man of a roving disposition, or for the stay-at-home, for that matter, for all roads lead to Hades. For instance, we do not find in previous guide-books, like Dante's Inferno, any references whatsoever to the languages it is well to know before taking the Stygian tour; to the kind of money needed, or its quantity per capita; no allusion to the necessity of passports is found in Dante or Virgil; custom-house requirements are ignored by these authors; no statements as to the kind of clothing needed, the quality of the hotels - nor indeed any real information of vital importance to the traveller is to be found in the older books. In Baedeker's Hades, on the other hand, all these subjects are exhaustively treated, together with a very comprehensive series of chapters on "Stygian Wines," "Climate," and "Hellish Art" - the expression is not mine - and other topics of essential interest.

And of what suggestive quality was this little book. Who would ever have guessed from a perusal of Dante that as

Hades is the place of departed spirits so also is it the ultimate resting-place of all other departed things. What delightful anticipations are there in the idea of a visit to the Alexandrian library, now suitably housed on the south side of Apollyon Square, Cimmeria, in a building that would drive the trustees of the Boston Public Library into envious despair, even though living Bacchantes are found daily improving their minds in the recesses of its commodious alcoves! What joyous feelings it gives one to think of visiting the navy-yards of Tyre and finding there the ships concerning the whereabouts of which poets have vainly asked questions for ages! Who would ever dream that the question of the balladist, himself an able dreamer concerning classic things, "Where are the Cities of Old Time," could ever find its answer in a simple guide-book telling us where Carthage is, where Troy and all the lost cities of antiquity!

Then the details of amusements in this wonderful country - who could gather aught of these from the Italian poet? The theatres of Gehenna, with "Hamlet" produced under the joint direction of Shakespeare and the Prince of Denmark himself, the great Zoo of Sheolia, with Jumbo, and the famous woolly horse of earlier days, not to mention the long series of menageries which have passed over the dark river in the ages now forgotten; the hanging gardens of Babylon, where the picnicking element of Hades flock week after week, chuting the chutes, and clambering joyously in and out of the Trojan Horse, now set up in all its majesty therein, with bowling-alleys on its roof, elevators in its legs, and the original Ferris-wheel in its head; the freak museums in the densely populated sections of the large cities, where Hop o' my Thumb and Jack the Giant Killer are exhibited day after day alongside of the great ogres they have killed; the opera-house, with Siegfried himself singing, supported by the real Brunhild and the original, bona fide dragon Fafnir, running of his own motive power, and breathing actual fire and smoke without the aid of a steam-engine and a plumber to connect him therewith before he can go out upon the stage to engage Siegfried in deadly combat.

For the information contained in this last item alone, even if the book had no other virtue, it would be worthy of careful perusal from the opening paragraph on language, to the last, dealing with the descent into the Vitriol Reservoir at Gehenna. The account of the feeding of Fafnir, to which admission can be had on payment of ten oboli, beginning with a puree of kerosene, followed by a half-dozen cartridges on the half-shell, an entree of nitro-glycerine, a solid roast of cannel-coal, and a salad of gun-cotton, with a mayonnaise dressing of alcohol and a pinch of powder, topped off with a demi-tasse of benzine and a box of matches to keep the fires of his spirit going, is one of the most moving things I have ever read, and yet it may be said without fear of contradiction that until this guide-book was prepared very few of the Stygian tourists have imagined that there was such a sight to be seen. I have gone carefully over Dante, Virgil, and the works of Andrew Lang, and have found no reference whatsoever in the pages of any of these talented persons to this marvellous spectacle which takes place three times a day, and which I doubt not results in a performance of Siegfried for the delectation of the music lovers of Hades, which is beyond the power of the human mind to conceive.

The hand-book has an added virtue, which distinguishes it from any other that I have ever seen, in that it is anecdotal in style at times where an anecdote is available and appropriate. In connection with this same Fafnir, as showing how necessary it is for the tourist to be careful of his personal safety in Hades, it is related that upon one occasion the keeper of the dragon having taken a grudge against Siegfried for some unintentional slight, fed Fafnir upon Roman-candles and a sky-rocket, with the result that in the fight between the hero and the demon of the wood the Siegfried was seriously injured by the red, white, and blue balls of fire which the dragon breathed out upon him, while the sky-rocket flew out into the audience and struck a young man in the top gallery, knocking him senseless, the stick falling into a grand-tier box and impaling one of the best known social lights of Cimmeria. "Therefore," adds the astute editor of the hand-book, "on Siegfried nights it were well if the tourist were to go provided with an asbestos umbrella for use in case of an emergency of a similar nature."

In that portion of the book devoted to the trip up the river Styx the legends surpass any of the Rhine stories in dramatic interest, because, according to Commodore Charon's excursion system, the tourist can step ashore and see the chief actors in them, who for a consideration will give a full-dress rehearsal of the legendary acts for which they have been famous. The sirens of the Stygian Lorelei, for instance, sit on an eminence not far above the city of Cimmeria, and make a profession of luring people ashore and giving away at so much per head locks of their hair for remembrance' sake, all of which makes of the Stygian trip a thing of far greater interest than that of the Rhine.

It had been my intention to make a few extracts from this portion of the volume showing later developments in the legends of the Drachenfels, and others of more than ordinary interest, but I find that with the departure of Boswell for the night the treasured hand-book disappeared with him; but, as I have already stated, if I can secure his consent to do so I will some day have the book copied off on more material substance than that employed in the original manuscript, so that the useful little tome may be printed and scattered broadcast over a waiting and appreciative world. I may as well state here, too, that I have taken the precaution to have the title "Baedeker's Hades" and its contents copyrighted, so that any pirate who recognizes the value of the scheme will attempt to pirate the work at his peril.

Hardly had I finished the chapter on the legends of the Styx when Boswell broke in upon me with: "Well, how do you like it?"

"It's great," I said. "May I keep it?"

"You may if you can," he laughed. "But I fancy it can't withstand the rigors of this climate any more than an unfireproof copy of one of your books could stand the caniculars of ours."

His words were soon to be verified, for as soon as he left me the book vanished, but whether it went off into thin air or was repocketed by the departing Boswell I am not entirely certain.

"What was it you asked me about Samson and Goliath?" Boswell observed, as he gathered up his manuscript from the floor beside the Enchanted Typewriter. "Whether they'd ever been in Honolulu?"

"No," I replied. "I got a letter from Hawaii the other day asking for the result of the prize-fight the day Kidd ran off with the house-boat."

"Oh," replied Boswell. "That? Why, ah, Samson won hands down, but only because they played according to latter-day rules. If it had been a regular knock-out fight, like the contests in the old days of the ring when it was in its prime, Goliath could have managed him with one hand; but the Samson backers played a sharp game on the Philistine by having the most recently amended Queensbury rules adopted, and Goliath wasn't in it five minutes after Samson opened his mouth."

"I don't think I understand," said I.

"Plain enough," explained Boswell. "Goliath didn't know what the modern rules were, but he thought a fight was a fight under any rules, so, like a decent chap, he agreed, and when he found that it was nothing but a talking-match he'd got into he fainted. He never was good at expressing himself fluently. Samson talked him down in two rounds, just as he did the other Philistines in the early days on earth."

I laughed. "You're slightly off there," I said. "That was a stand-up-and-be-knocked-down fight, wasn't it? He used the jawbone of an ass?"

"Very true," observed Boswell, "but it is evident that it is you who are slightly off. You haven't kept up with the higher criticism. It has been proven scientifically that not only did the whale not swallow Jonah, but that Samson's great feat against the Philistines was comparable only to the achievements of your modern senators. He talked them to death."

"Then why jawbone of an ass?" I cried.

"Samson was an ass," replied Boswell. "They prove that

by the temple episode, for you see if he hadn't been one he'd have got out of the building before yanking the foundations from under it. I tell you, old chap, this higher criticism is a great thing, and as logical as death itself."

And with this Boswell left me.

I sincerely hope that the result of the fight will prove as satisfactory to my friend in Hawaii as it was to me; for while I have no particular admiration for Samson, I have always rejoiced to hear of the discomfitures of Goliath, who, so far as I have been able to ascertain, was not only not a gentleman, but, in addition, had no more regard for the rights of others than a member of the New York police force or the editor of a Sunday newspaper with a thirst for sensation.

IX

SHERLOCK HOLMES AGAIN

I had intended asking Boswell what had become of my copy of the Baedeker's Hades when he next returned, but the output of the machine that evening so interested me that the hand-book was entirely forgotten. If there ever was a hero in this world who could compare with D'Artagnan in my estimation for sheer ability in a given line that hero was Sherlock Holmes. With D'Artagnan and Holmes for my companions I think I could pass the balance of my days in absolute contentment, no matter what woful things might befall me. So it was that, when I next heard the tapping keys and dulcet bell of my Enchanted Type-writer, and, after listening intently for a moment, realized that my friend Boswell was making a copy of a Sherlock Holmes Memoir thereon for his next Sunday's paper, all thought of the interesting little red book of the last meeting flew out of my head. I rose quickly from my couch at the first sounding of the gong.

"Got a Holmes story, eh?" I said, walking to his side, and gazing eagerly over the spot where his shoulder should have been.

"I have that, and it's a winner," he replied, enthusiastically. "If you don't believe it, read it. I'll have it copied in about two minutes."

"I'll do both," I said. "I believe all the Sherlock Holmes stories I read. It is so much pleasanter to believe them true. If they weren't true they wouldn't be so wonderful."

With this I picked up the first page of the manuscript and shortly after Boswell presented me with the balance, whereon I read the following extraordinary tale:

A MYSTERY SOLVED

A WONDERFUL ACHIEVEMENT IN FERRETING

From Advance Sheets of

MEMOIRS I REMEMBER

BY

SHERLOCK HOLMES, ESQ.

Ferreter Extraordinary by Special Appointment to his Majesty Apollyon

- - - - - - - --

WHO THE LADY WAS!

It was not many days after my solution of the Missing Diamond of the Nizam of Jigamaree Mystery that I was called upon to take up a case which has baffled at least one person for some ten or eleven centuries. The reader will remember the mystery of the missing diamond - the largest known in all history, which the Nizam of Jigamaree brought from India to present to the Queen of England, on the occasion of her diamond jubilee. I had been dead three years at the time, but, by a special dispensation of his Imperial Highness Apollyon, was permitted to return incog to London for the jubilee season, where it so happened that I put up at the same lodging-house as that occupied by the Nizam and his suite. We sat opposite each other at table d'hote, and for at least three weeks previous to the losing of his treasure the Indian prince was very morose, and it was very difficult to get him to speak. I was not supposed to know, nor, indeed, was any one else, for that matter, at the lodging-house, that the Nizam was so exalted a personage. He like myself was travelling incog and was known to the world as Mr. Wilkins, of Calcutta - a very wise precaution, inasmuch as he had in his possession a gem valued at a million and a half of dollars. I recognized him at once, however, by his unlikeness to a wood-cut that had been appearing in the American Sunday newspapers, labelled with his name, as well as by the extraordinary lantern which he had on his bicycle, a lantern which to the uneducated eye was no more than an ordinary lamp, but which to an eye like mine, familiar with gems, had for its crystal lens nothing more nor less than the famous stone which he had brought for her Majesty the Queen, his imperial sovereign. There are few people who can tell diamonds from plate-glass under any circumstances, and Mr. Wilkins, otherwise the Nizam, realizing this fact, had taken this bold method of secreting his treasure. Of course, the moment I perceived the quality of the man's lamp I knew at once who Mr. Wilkins was, and I determined to have a little innocent diversion at his expense.

"It has been a fine day, Mr. Wilkins," said I one evening over the pate.

"Yes," he replied, wearily. "Very - but somehow or other I'm depressed to-night."

"Too bad," I said, lightly, "but there are others. There's that poor Nizam of Jigamaree, for instance - poor devil, he must be the bluest brown man that ever lived."

Wilkins started nervously as I mentioned the prince by name.

"Wh-why do you think that?" he asked, nervously fingering his butter-knife.

"It's tough luck to have to give away a diamond that's worth three or four times as much as the Koh-i-noor," I said. "Suppose you owned a stone like that. Would you care to give it away?"

"Not by a damn sight!" cried Wilkins, forcibly, and I noticed great tears gathering in his eyes.

"Still, he can't help himself, I suppose," I said, gazing abruptly at his scarf-pin. "That is, he doesn't KNOW that he can. The Queen expects it. It's been announced, and now the poor devil can't get out of it - though I'll tell you, Mr. Wilkins, if I were the Nizam of Jigamaree, I'd get out of it in ten seconds."

I winked at him significantly. He looked at me blankly.

"Yes, sir," I added, merely to arouse him, "in just ten seconds! Ten short, beautiful seconds."

"Mr. Postlethwaite," said the Nizam - Postlethwaite was the name I was travelling under - "Mr. Postlethwaite," said the Nizam - otherwise Wilkins - "your remarks interest me greatly." His face wreathed with a smile that I had never before seen there. "I have thought as you do in regard to this poor Indian prince, but I must confess I don't see how he can get out of giving the Queen that diamond. Have a cigar, Mr. Postlethwaite, and, waiter, bring us a triple magnum of champagne. Do you really think, Mr. Postlethwaite, that there is a way out of it? If you would like a ticket to Westminster for the ceremony, there are a half-dozen."

He tossed six tickets for seats among the crowned heads across the table to me. His eagerness was almost too painful to witness.

"Thank you," said I, calmly pocketing the tickets, for they were of rare value at that time. "The way out of it is very simple."

"Indeed, Mr. Postlethwaite," said he, trying to keep cool. "Ah - are you interested in rubies, sir? There are a few which I should be pleased to have you accept" - and with that over came a handful of precious stones each worth a fortune. These also I pocketed as I replied:

"Why, certainly; if I were the Nizam," said I, "I'd lose that diamond."

A shade of disappointment came over Mr. Wilkins's face.

"Lose it? How? Where?" he asked, with a frown.

"Yes. Lose it. Any way I could. As for the place where it should be lost, any old place will do as long as it is where he can find it again when he gets back home. He might leave it in his other clothes, or -"

"Make that two triple magnums, waiter," cried Mr. Wilkins, excitedly, interrupting me. "Postlethwaite, you're a genius, and if you ever want a house and lot in

Calcutta, just let me know and they're yours."

You never saw such a change come over a man in all your life. Where he had been all gloom before, he was now all smiles and jollity, and from that time on to his return to India Mr. Wilkins was as happy as a school-boy at the beginning of vacation. The next day the diamond was lost, and whoever may have it at this moment, the British Crown is not in possession of the Jigamaree gem.

But, as my friend Terence Mulvaney says, that is another story. It is of the mystery immediately following this concerning which I have set out to write.

I was sitting one day in my office on Apollyon Square opposite the Alexandrian library, smoking an absinthe cigarette, which I had rolled myself from my special mixture consisting of two parts tobacco, one part hasheesh, one part of opium dampened with a liqueur glass of absinthe, when an excited knock sounded upon my door.

"Come in," I cried, adopting the usual formula.

The door opened and a beautiful woman stood before me clad in most regal garments, robust of figure, yet extremely pale. It seemed to me that I had seen her somewhere before, yet for a time I could not place her.

"Mr. Sherlock Holmes?" said she, in deliciously musical tones, which, singular to relate, she emitted in a fashion suggestive of a recitative passage in an opera.

"The same," said I, bowing with my accustomed courtesy.

"The ferret?" she sang, in staccato tones which were ravishing to my musical soul.

I laughed. "That term has been applied to me, madame," said I, chanting my answer as best I could. "For myself, however, I prefer to assume the more modest title of detective. I can work with or without clues, and have never yet been baffled. I know who wrote the Junius letters, and upon occasions have been known to see through a stone wall with my naked eye. What can I do for you?"

"Tell me who I am!" she cried, tragically, taking the centre of the room and gesticulating wildly.

"Well - really, madame," I replied. "You didn't send up any card -"

"Ah!" she sneered. "This is what your vaunted prowess amounts to, eh? Ha! Do you suppose if I had a card with my name on it I'd have come to you to inquire who I am? I can read a card as well as you can, Mr. Sherlock Holmes."

"Then, as I understand it, madame," I put in, "you have suddenly forgotten your identity and wish me to -"

"Nothing of the sort. I have forgotten nothing. I never knew for certain who I am. I have an impression, but it is based only on hearsay evidence," she interrupted.

For a moment I was fairly puzzled. Still I did not wish to let her know this, and so going behind my screen and taking a capsule full of cocaine to steady my nerves, I gained a moment to think. Returning, I said:

"This really is child's play for me, madame. It won't take more than a week to find out who you are, and possibly, if you have any clews at all to your identity, I may be able to solve this mystery in a day."

"I have only three," she answered, and taking a piece of swan's-down, a lock of golden hair, and a pair of silver-tinsel tights from her portmanteau she handed them over to me.

My first impulse was to ask the lady if she remembered the name of the asylum from which she had escaped, but I fortunately refrained from doing so, and she shortly left me, promising to return at the end of the week.

For three days I puzzled over the clews. Swan's-down, yellow hair, and a pair of silver-tinsel tights, while very interesting no doubt at times, do not form a very solid basis for a theory establishing the identity of so regal a person as my visitor. My first impression was that she was a vaudeville artist, and that the exhibits she had left me were a part of her make-up. This I was forced to abandon shortly, because no woman with the voice of my visitor would sing in vaudeville. The more ambitious stage was her legitimate field, if not grand opera itself.

At this point she returned to my office, and I of course reported progress. That is one of the most valuable things I learned while on earth - when you have done nothing, report progress.

"I haven't quite succeeded as yet," said I, "but I am getting at it slowly. I do not, however, think it wise to acquaint you with my present notions until they are verified beyond peradventure. It might help me somewhat if you were to tell me who it is you think you

John Kendrick Bangs

are. I could work either forward or backward on that hypothesis, as seemed best, and so arrive at a hypothetical truth anyhow."

"That's just what I don't want to do," said she. "That information might bias your final judgment. If, however, acting on the clews which you have, you confirm my impression that I am such and such a person, as well as the views which other people have, then will my status be well defined and I can institute my suit against my husband for a judicial separation, with back alimony, with some assurance of a successful issue."

I was more puzzled than ever.

"Well," said I, slowly, "I of course can see how a bit of swan's-down and a lock of yellow hair backed up by a pair of silver-tinsel tights might constitute reasonable evidence in a suit for separation, but wouldn't it - ah - be more to your purpose if I should use these data as establishing the identity of - er - somebody else?"

"How very dense you are," she replied, impatiently. "That's precisely what I want you to do."

"But you told me it was your identity you wished proven," I put in, irritably.

"Precisely," said she.

"Then these bits of evidence are - yours?" I asked, hesitatingly. One does not like to accuse a lady of an undue liking for tinsel.

"They are all I have left of my husband," she answered with a sob.

"Hum!" said I, my perplexity increasing. "Was the - ah - the gentleman blown up by dynamite?"

"Excuse me, Mr. Holmes," she retorted, rising and running the scales. "I think, after all, I have come to the wrong shop. Have you Hawkshaw's address handy? You are too obtuse for a detective."

My reputation was at stake, so I said, significantly:

"Good! Good! I was merely trying one of my disguises on you, madame, and you were completely taken in. Of course no one would ever know me for Sherlock Holmes if I manifested such dullness."

"Ah!" she said, her face lighting up. "You were merely deceiving me by appearing to be obtuse?"

"Of course," said I. "I see the whole thing in a nutshell. You married an adventurer; he told you who he was, but you've never been able to prove it; and suddenly you are deserted by him, and on going over his wardrobe you find he has left nothing but these articles: and now you wish to sue him for a separation on the ground of desertion, and secure alimony if possible."

It was a magnificent guess.

"That is it precisely," said the lady. "Except as to the extent of his 'leavings.' In addition to the things you have he gave my small brother a brass bugle and a tin sword."

"We may need to see them later," said I. "At present I will do all I can for you on the evidence in hand. I have got my eye on a gentleman who wears silver-tinsel tights now, but I am afraid he is not the man we are after, because his hair is black, and, as far as I have been able to learn from his valet, he is utterly unacquainted with swan's-down."

We separated again and I went to the club to think. Never in my life before had I had so baffling a case. As I sat in the cafe sipping a cocaine cobbler, who should walk in but Hamlet, strangely enough picking particles of swan's-down from his black doublet, which was literally covered with it.

"Hello, Sherlock!" he said, drawing up a chair and sitting down beside me. "What you up to?"

"Trying to make out where you have been," I replied. "I judge from the swan's-down on your doublet that you have been escorting Ophelia to the opera in the regulation cloak."

"You're mistaken for once," he laughed. "I've been driving with Lohengrin. He's got a pair of swans that can do a mile in 2.10 - but it makes them moult like the devil."

"Pair of what?" I cried.

"Swans," said Hamlet. "He's an eccentric sort of a duffer, that Lohengrin. Afraid of horses, I fancy."

"And so drives swans instead?" said I, incredulously.

"The same," replied Hamlet. "Do I look as if he drove squab?"

"He must be queer," said I. "I'd like to meet him. He'd make quite an addition to my collection of freaks."

"Very well," observed Hamlet. "He'll be here to-morrow to take luncheon with me, and if you'll come, too, you'll be most welcome. He's collecting freaks, too, and I haven't a doubt would be pleased to know you."

We parted and I sauntered homeward, cogitating over my strange client, and now and then laughing over the idiosyncrasies of Hamlet's friend the swan-driver. It never occurred to me at the moment however to connect the two, in spite of the link of swan's-down. I regarded it merely as a coincidence. The next day, however, on going to the club and meeting Hamlet's strange guest, I was struck by the further coincidence that his hair was of precisely the same shade of yellow as that in my possession. It was of a hue that I had never seen before except at performances of grand opera, or on the heads of fool detectives in musical burlesques. Here, however, was the real thing growing luxuriantly from the man's head.

"Ho-ho!" thought I to myself. "Here is a fortunate encounter; there may be something in it," and then I tried to lead him on.

"I understand, Mr. Lohengrin," I said, "that you have a fine span of swans."

"Yes," he said, and I was astonished to note that he, like my client, spoke in musical numbers. "Very. They're much finer than horses, in my opinion. More peaceful, quite as rapid, and amphibious. If I go out for a drive and come to a lake they trot quite as well across its surface as on the highways."

"How interesting!" said I. "And so gentle, the swan. Your wife, I presume -"

Hamlet kicked my shins under the table.

"I think it will rain to-morrow," he said, giving me a glance which if it said anything said shut up.

"I think so, too," said Lohengrin, a lowering look on his face. "If it doesn't, it will either snow, or hail, or be clear." And he gazed abstractedly out of the window.

The kick and the man's confusion were sufficient proof. I was on the right track at last. Yet the evidence was unsatisfactory because merely circumstantial. My piece of down might have come from an opera cloak and not from a well-broken swan, the hair might equally clearly have come from some other head than Lohengrin's, and other men have had trouble with their wives. The circumstantial evidence lying in the coincidences was strong but not conclusive, so I resolved to pursue the matter and invite the strange individual to a luncheon with me, at which I proposed to wear the tinsel tights. Seeing them, he might be forced into betraying himself.

This I did, and while my impressions were confirmed by his demeanor, no positive evidence grew out of it.

"I'm hungry as a bear!" he said, as I entered the club, clad in a long, heavy ulster, reaching from my shoulders to the ground, so that the tights were not visible.

"Good," said I. "I like a hearty eater," and I ordered a luncheon of ten courses before removing my overcoat; but not one morsel could the man eat, for on the removal of my coat his eye fell upon my silver garments, and with a gasp he wellnigh fainted. It was clear. He recognized them and was afraid, and in consequence lost his appetite. But he was game, and tried to laugh it off.

"Silver man, I see," he said, nervously, smiling.

"No," said I, taking the lock of golden hair from my pocket and dangling it before him. "Bimetallist."

His jaw dropped in dismay, but recovering himself instantly he put up a fairly good fight.

"It is strange, Mr. Lohengrin," said I, "that in the three years I have been here I've never seen you before."

"I've been very quiet," he said. "Fact is, I have had my reasons, Mr. Holmes, for preferring the life of a hermit. A youthful indiscretion, sir, has made me fear to face the world. There was nothing wrong about it, save that it was a folly, and I have been anxious in these days of newspapers to avoid any possible revival of what might in some eyes seem scandalous."

I felt sorry for him, but my duty was clear. Here was my man - but how to gain direct proof was still beyond me. No further admissions could be got out of him, and we soon parted.

Two days later the lady called and again I reported progress.

"It needs but one thing, madame, to convince me that I have found your husband," said I. "I have found a man who might be connected with swan's-down, from whose luxuriant curls might have come this tow-colored lock, and who might have worn the silver-tinsel tights - yet it is all MIGHT and no certainty."

"I will bring my small brother's bugle and the tin sword," said she. "The sword has certain properties which may induce him to confess. My brother tells me that if he simply shakes it at a cat the cat falls dead."

"Do so," said I, "and I will try it on him. If he recognizes the sword and remembers its properties when I attempt to brandish it at him, he'll be forced to confess, though it would be awkward if he is the wrong man and the sword should work on him as it does on the cat."

The next day I was in possession of the famous toy. It was not very long, and rather more suggestive of a pancake-turner than a sword, but it was a terror. I tested its qualities on a swarm of gnats in my room, and the moment I shook it at them they fluttered to the ground as dead as door-nails.

"I'll have to be careful of this weapon," I thought. "It would be terrible if I should brandish it at a motor-man trying to get one of the Gehenna Traction Company's cable-cars to stop and he should drop dead at his post."

All was now ready for the demonstration. Fortunately the following Saturday night was club night at the House-Boat, and we were all expected to come in costume. For dramatic effect I wore a yellow wig, a helmet, the silver-tinsel tights, and a doublet to match, with the brass bugle and the tin sword properly slung about my person. I looked stunning, even if I do say it, and much to my surprise several people mistook me for the man I was after. Another link in the chain! EVEN THE PUBLIC UNCONSCIOUSLY RECOGNIZED THE VALUE OF MY DEDUCTIONS. THEY CALLED ME LOHENGRIN!

And of course it all happened as I expected. It always does. Lohengrin came into the assembly-room five minutes after I did and was visibly annoyed at my make-up.

"This is a great liberty," said he, grasping the hilt of his sword; but I answered by blowing the bugle at him, at which he turned livid and fell back. He had recognized its soft cadence. I then hauled the sword from my belt, shook it at a fly on the wall, which immediately died, and made as if to do the same at Lohengrin, whereupon he cried for mercy and fell upon his knees.

"Turn that infernal thing the other way!" he shrieked.

"Ah!" said I, lowering my arm. "Then you know its properties?"

"I do - I do!" he cried. "It used to be mine - I confess it!"

"Then," said I, calmly putting the horrid bit of zinc back into my belt, "that's all I wanted to know. If you'll come up to my office some morning next week I'll introduce you to your wife," and I turned from him.

My mission accomplished, I left the festivities and returned to my quarters where my fair client was awaiting me.

"Well?" she said.

"It's all right, Mrs. Lohengrin," I said, and the lady cried aloud with joy at the name, for it was the very one she had hoped it would be. "My man turns out to be your man, and I turn him over therefore to you, only deal gently with him. He's a pretty decent chap and sings like a bird."

Whereon I presented her with my bill for 5000 oboli, which she paid without a murmur, as was entirely proper that she should, for upon the evidence which I had secured the fair plaintiff, in the suit for separation of Elsa vs. Lohengrin on the ground of desertion and non-support, obtained her decree, with back alimony of twenty-five per cent. of Lohengrin's income for a trifle over fifteen hundred years.

How much that amounted to I really do not know, but that it was a large sum I am sure, for Lohengrin must have been very wealthy. He couldn't have afforded to dress in solid silver-tinsel tights if he had been otherwise. I had the tights assayed before returning them to their owner, and even in a country where free coinage of tights is looked upon askance they could not be duplicated for less than $850 at a ratio of 32 to 1.

CHAPTER X

GOLF IN HADES

"Jim," said I to Boswell one morning as the type-writer began to work, "perhaps you can enlighten me on a point concerning which a great many people have questioned me recently. Has golf taken hold of Hades yet? You referred to it some time ago, and I've been wondering ever since if it had become a fad with you."

"Has it?" laughed my visitor; "well, I should rather say it had. The fact is, it has been a great boon to the country. You remember my telling you of the projected revolution led by Cromwell, and Caesar, and the others?"

"I do, very well," said I, "and I have been intending to ask you how it came out."

"Oh, everything's as fine and sweet as can be now," rejoined Boswell, somewhat gleefully, "and all because of golf. We are all quiet along the Styx now. All animosities are buried in the general love of golf, and every one of us, high or low, autocrat and revolutionist, is hobnobbing away in peace and happiness on the links. Why, only six weeks ago, Apollyon was for cooking Bonaparte on a waffle iron, and yesterday the two went out to the Cimmerian links together and played a mixed foursome,

Bonaparte and Medusa playing against Apollyon and Delilah."

"Dear me! Really?" I cried. "That must have been an interesting match."

"It was, and up to the very last it was nip-and-tuck between 'em," said Boswell. "Apollyon and Delilah won it with one hole up, and they got that on the put. They'd have halved the hole if Medusa's back hair hadn't wiggled loose and bitten her caddie just as she was holeing out."

"It is a remarkable game," said I. "There is no sensation in the world quite equal to that which comes to a man's soul when he has hit the ball a solid clip and sees it sail off through the air towards the green, whizzing musically along like a very bird."

"True," said Boswell; "but I'm rather of the opinion that it's a safer game for shades than for you purely material persons."

"I don't see why," I answered.

"It is easy to understand," returned Boswell. "For instance, with us there is no resistance when by a mischance we come into unexpected contact with the ball. Take the experience of Diogenes and Solomon at the St. Jonah's Links week before last. The Wiseman's Handicap was on. Diogenes and Simple Simon were playing just ahead of Solomon and Montaigne. Solomon was driving in great form. For the first time in his life he seemed able to keep his eye on the ball, and the way he sent it flying through the air was a caution. Diogenes and Simple Simon had both had their second stroke and

Solomon drove off. His ball sailed straight ahead like a missile from a catapult, flew in a bee-line for Diogenes, struck him at the base of his brain, continued on through, and landed on the edge of the green."

"Mercy!" I cried. "Didn't it kill him?"

"Of course not," retorted Boswell. "You can't kill a shade. Diogenes didn't know he'd been hit, but if that had happened to one of you material golfers there'd have been a sickening end to that tournament."

"There would, indeed," said I. "There isn't much fun in being hit by a golf-ball. I can testify to that because I have had the experience," and I called to mind the day at St. Peterkin's when I unconsciously stymied with my material self the celebrated Willie McGuffin, the Demon Driver from the Hootmon Links, Scotland. McGuffin made his mark that day if he never did before, and I bear the evidence thereof even now, although the incident took place two years ago, when I did not know enough to keep out of the way of the player who plays so well that he thinks he has a perpetual right of way everywhere.

"What kind of clubs do you Stygians use?" I asked.

"Oh, very much the same kind that you chaps do," returned Boswell. "Everybody experiments with new fads, too, just as you do. Old Peter Stuyvesant, for instance, always drives with his wooden leg, and never uses anything else unless he gets a lie where he's got to."

"His wooden leg?" I roared, with a laugh. "How on earth does he do that?"

"He screws the small end of it into a square block shod

John Kendrick Bangs

like a brassey," explained Boswell, "tees up his ball, goes back ten yards, makes a run at it and kicks the ball pretty nearly out of sight. He can put with it too, like a dream, swinging it sideways."

"But he doesn't call that golf, does he?" I cried.

"What is it?" demanded Boswell.

"I should call it football," I said.

"Not at all," said Boswell. "Not a bit of it. He hasn't any foot on that leg, and he has a golf-club head with a shaft to it. There isn't any rule which says that the shaft shall not look like an inverted nine-pin, nor do any of the accepted authorities require that the club shall be manipulated by the arms. I admit it's bad form the way he plays, but, as Stuyvesant himself says, he never did travel on his shape."

"Suppose he gets a cuppy lie?" I asked, very much interested at the first news from Hades of the famous old Dutchman.

"Oh, he does one of two things," said Boswell. "He stubs it out with his toe, or goes back and plays two more. Munchausen plays a good game too. He beat the colonel forty-seven straight holes last Wednesday, and all Hades has been talking about it ever since."

"Who is the colonel?" I asked, innocently.

"Bogey," returned Boswell. "Didn't you ever hear of Colonel Bogey?"

"Of course," I replied, "but I always supposed Bogey was

an imaginary opponent, not a real one."

"So he is," said Boswell.

"Then you mean -"

"I mean that Munchausen beat him forty-seven up," said Boswell.

"Were there any witnesses?" I demanded, for I had little faith in Munchausen's regard for the eternal verities, among which a golf-card must be numbered if the game is to survive.

"Yes, a hundred," said Boswell. "There was only one trouble with 'em." Here the great biographer laughed. "They were all imaginary, like the colonel."

"And Munchausen's score?" I queried.

"The same, naturally. But it makes him king-pin in golf circles just the same, because nobody can go back on his logic," said Boswell. "Munchausen reasoned it out very logically indeed, and largely, he said, to protect his own reputation. Here is an imaginary warrior, said he, who makes a bully, but wholly imaginary, score at golf. He sends me an imaginary challenge to play him forty-seven holes. I accept, not so much because I consider myself a golfer as because I am an imaginer - if there is such a word."

"Ask Dr. Johnson," said I, a little sarcastically. I always grow sarcastic when golf is mentioned.

"Dr. Johnson be -" began Boswell.

"Boswell!" I remonstrated.

"Dr. Johnson be it, I was about to say," clicked the type-writer, suavely; but the ink was thick and inclined to spread. "Munchausen felt that Bogey was encroaching on his preserve as a man with an imagination."

"I have always considered Colonel Bogey a liar," said I. "He joins all the clubs and puts up an ideal score before he has played over the links."

"That isn't the point at all," said Boswell. "Golfers don't lie. Realists don't lie. Nobody in polite - or say, rather, accepted - society lies. They all imagine. Munchausen realizes that he has only one claim to recognition, and that is based entirely upon his imagination. So when the imaginary Colonel Bogey sent him an imaginary challenge to play him forty-seven holes at golf -"

"Why forty-seven?" I asked.

"An imaginary number," explained Boswell. "Don't interrupt. As I say, when the imaginary colonel -"

"I must interrupt," said I. "What was he colonel of?"

"A regiment of perfect caddies," said Boswell.

"Ah, I see," I replied. "Imaginary in his command. There isn't one perfect caddy, much less a regiment of the little reprobates."

"You are wrong there," said Boswell. "You don't know how to produce a good caddy - but good caddies can be made."

"How?" I cried, for I have suffered. "I'll have the plan patented."

"Take a flexible brassey, and at the ninth hole, if they deserve it, give them eighteen strokes across the legs with all your strength," said Boswell. "But, as I said before, don't interrupt. I haven't much time left to talk with you."

"But I must ask one more question," I put in, for I was growing excited over a new idea. "You say give them eighteen strokes across the legs. Across whose legs?"

"Yours," replied Boswell. "Just take your caddy up, place him across your knees, and spank him with your brassey. Spank isn't a good golf term, but it is good enough for the average caddy; in fact, it will do him good."

"Go on," said I, with a mental resolve to adopt his prescription.

"Well," said Boswell, "Munchausen, having received an imaginary challenge from an imaginary opponent, accepted. He went out to the links with an imaginary ball, an imaginary bagful of fanciful clubs, and licked the imaginary life out of the colonel."

"Still, I don't see," said I, somewhat jealously, perhaps, "how that makes him king-pin in golf circles. Where did he play?"

"On imaginary links," said Boswell.

"Poh!" I ejaculated.

"Don't sneer," said Boswell. "You know yourself that the

John Kendrick Bangs

links you imagine are far better than any others."

"What is Munchausen's strongest point?" I asked, seeing that there was no arguing with the man - "driving, approaching, or putting?"

"None of the three. He cannot put, he foozles every drive, and at approaching he's a consummate ass," said Boswell.

"Then what can he do?" I cried.

"Count," said Boswell. "Haven't you learned that yet? You can spend hours learning how to drive, weeks to approach, and months to put. But if you want to win you must know how to count."

I was silent, and for the first time in my life I realized that Munchausen was not so very different from certain golfers I have met in my short day as a golfiac, and then Boswell put in:

"You see, it isn't lofting or driving that wins," he continued. "Cups aren't won on putting or approaching. It's the man who puts in the best card who becomes the champion."

"I am afraid you are right," I said, sadly, "but I am sorry to find that Hades is as badly off as we mortals in that matter."

"Golf, sir," retorted Boswell, sententiously, "is the same everywhere, and that which is dome in our world is directly in line with what is developed in yours."

"I'm sorry for Hades," said I; "but to continue about golf

- do the ladies play much on your links?"

"Well, rather," returned Boswell, "and it's rather amusing to watch them at it, too. Xanthippe with her Greek clothes finds it rather difficult; but for rare sport you ought to see Queen Elizabeth trying to keep her eye on the ball over her ruff! It really is one of the finest spectacles you ever saw."

"But why don't they dress properly?"

"Ah," sighed Boswell, "that is one of the things about Hades that destroys all the charm of life there. We are but shades."

"Granted," said I, "but your garments can -"

"Our garments can't," said Boswell. "Through all eternity we shades of our former selves are doomed to wear the shadows of our former clothes."

"Then what the devil does a poor dress-maker do who goes to Hades?" I cried.

"She makes over the things she made before," said Boswell. "That's why, my dear fellow," the biographer added, becoming confidential - "that's why some people confound Hades with - ah - the other place, don't you know."

"Still, there's golf!" I said; "and that's a panacea for all ills. YOU enjoy it, don't you?"

"Me?" cried Boswell. "Me enjoy it? Not on all the lives in Christendom. It is the direst drudgery for me."

John Kendrick Bangs

"Drudgery?" I said. "Bah! Nonsense, Boswell!"

"You forget -" he began.

"Forget? It must be you who forget, if you call golf drudgery."

"No," sighed the genial spirit. "No, *I* don't forget. I remember."

"Remember what?" I demanded.

"That I am Dr. Johnson's caddy!" was the answer. And then came a heart-rending sigh, and from that time on all was silence. I repeatedly put questions to the machine, made observations to it, derided it, insulted it, but there was no response.

It has so continued to this day, and I can only conclude the story of my Enchanted Type-writer by saying that I presume golf has taken the same hold upon Hades that it has upon this world, and that I need not hope to hear more from that attractive region until the game has relaxed its grip, which I know can never be.

Hence let me say to those who have been good enough to follow me through the realms of the Styx that I bid them an affectionate farewell and thank them for their kind attention to my chronicles. They are all truthful; but now that the source of supply is cut off I cannot prove it. I can only hope that for one and all the future may hold as much of pleasure as the place of departed spirits has held for me.

Choose from Thousands of 1stWorldLibrary Classics By

Adolphus WilliamWard
Aesop
Agatha Christie
Alexander Aaronsohn
Alexander Kielland
Alexandre Dumas
Alfred Gatty
Alfred Ollivant
Alice Duer Miller
Alice Turner Curtis
Alice Dunbar
Ambrose Bierce
Amelia E. Barr
Andrew Lang
Andrew McFarland Davis
Anna Sewell
Annie Besant
Annie Hamilton Donnell
Annie Payson Call
Anton Chekhov
Arnold Bennett
Arthur Conan Doyle
Arthur Ransome
Atticus
B. M. Bower
Basil King
Bayard Taylor
Ben Macomber
Booth Tarkington
Bram Stoker
C. Collodi
C. E. Orr
C. M. Ingleby
Carolyn Wells
Catherine Parr Traill
Charles A. Eastman
Charles Dickens
Charles Dudley Warner
Charles Farrar Browne
Charles Ives
Charles Kingsley
Charles Lathrop Pack
Charles Whibley
Charles Willing Beale
Charlotte M. Braeme
Charlotte M.Yonge
Clair W. Hayes
Clarence Day Jr.
Clarence E. Mulford

Clemence Housman
Confucius
Cornelis DeWitt Wilcox
Cyril Burleigh
D. H. Lawrence
Daniel Defoe
David Garnett
Don Carlos Janes
Donald Keyhole
Dorothy Kilner
Dougan Clark
E. Nesbit
E.P.Roe
E. Phillips Oppenheim
Edgar Allan Poe
Edgar Rice Burroughs
Edith Wharton
Edward J. O'Biren
John Cournos
Edwin L. Arnold
Eleanor Atkins
Elizabeth Cleghorn
Gaskell
Elizabeth Von Arnim
Ellem Key
Emily Dickinson
Erasmus W. Jones
Ernie Howard Pie
Ethel Turner
Ethel Watts Mumford
Eugenie Foa
Eugene Wood
Evelyn Everett-Green
Everard Cotes
F. J. Cross
Federick Austin Ogg
Ferdinand Ossendowski
Francis Bacon
Francis Darwin
Frances Hodgson Burnett
Frank Gee Patchin
Frank Harris
Frank Jewett Mather
Frank L. Packard
Frederick Trevor Hill
Frederick Winslow Taylor
Friedrich Kerst
Friedrich Nietzsche
Fyodor Dostoyevsky

Gabrielle E. Jackson
Garrett P. Serviss
Gaston Leroux
George Ade
Geroge Bernard Shaw
George Ebers
George Eliot
George MacDonald
George Orwell
George Tucker
George W. Cable
George Wharton James
Gertrude Atherton
Grace E. King
Grant Allen
Guillermo A. Sherwell
Gulielma Zollinger
Gustav Flaubert
H. A. Cody
H. B. Irving
H. G. Wells
H. H. Munro
H. Irving Hancock
H. Rider Haggard
H. W. C. Davis
Hamilton Wright Mabie
Hans Christian Andersen
Harold Avery
Harold McGrath
Harriet Beecher Stowe
Harry Houidini
Helent Hunt Jackson
Helen Nicolay
Hendy David Thoreau
Henrik Ibsen
Henry Adams
Henry Ford
Henry Frost
Henry James
Henry Jones Ford
Henry Seton Merriman
Henry Wadsworth
Longfellow
Henry W Longfellow
Herbert A. Giles
Herbert N. Casson
Herman Hesse
Homer
Honore De Balzac

Horace Walpole
Horatio Alger, Jr.
Howard Pyle
Howard R. Garis
Hugh Lofting
Hugh Walpole
Humphry Ward
Ian Maclaren
Israel Abrahams
J.G.Austin
J. Henri Fabre
J. M. Barrie
J. Macdonald Oxley
J. S. Knowles
J. Storer Clouston
Jack London
Jacob Abbott
James Allen
James Lane Allen
James Andrews
James Baldwin
James DeMille
James Joyce
James Oliver Curwood
James Oppenheim
James Otis
Jane Austen
Jens Peter Jacobsen
Jerome K. Jerome
John Burroughs
John F. Kennedy
John Gay
John Glasworthy
John Habberton
John Joy Bell
John Milton
John Philip Sousa
Jonathan Swift
Joseph Carey
Joseph Conrad
Joseph Jacobs
Julian Hawthrone
Julies Vernes
Justin Huntly McCarthy
Kakuzo Okakura
Kenneth Grahame
Kate Langley Bosher
L. A. Abbot
L. T. Meade
L. Frank Baum
Laura Lee Hope

Laurence Housman
Leo Tolstoy
Leonid Andreyev
Lewis Carroll
Lilian Bell
Lloyd Osbourne
Louis Tracy
Louisa May Alcott
Lucy Fitch Perkins
Lucy Maud Montgomery
Lydia Miller Middleton
Lyndon Orr
M. H. Adams
Margaret E. Sangster
Margaret Vandercook
Maria Edgeworth
Maria Thompson Daviess
Mariano Azuela
Marion Polk Angellotti
Mark Overton
Mark Twain
Mary Austin
Mary Cole
Mary Rowlandson
Mary Wollstonecraft
Shelley
Max Beerbohm
Myra Kelly
Nathaniel Hawthrone
O. F. Walton
Oscar Wilde
Owen Johnson
P.G.Wodehouse
Paul and Mable Thorn
Paul G. Tomlinson
Paul Severing
Peter B. Kyne
Plato
R. Derby Holmes
R. L. Stevenson
Rabindranath Tagore
Rahul Alvares
Ralph Waldo Emmerson
Rene Descartes
Rex E. Beach
Richard Harding Davis
Richard Jefferies
Robert Barr
Robert Frost
Robert Gordon Anderson
Robert L. Drake

Robert Lansing
Robert Michael Ballantyne
Robert W. Chambers
Rosa Nouchette Carey
Ross Kay
Rudyard Kipling
Samuel B. Allison
Samuel Hopkins Adams
Sarah Bernhardt
Selma Lagerlof
Sherwood Anderson
Sigmund Freud
Standish O'Grady
Stanley Weyman
Stella Benson
Stephen Crane
Stewart Edward White
Stijn Streuvels
Swami Abhedananda
Swami Parmananda
T. S. Ackland
The Princess Der Ling
Thomas A. Janvier
Thomas A Kempis
Thomas Anderton
Thomas Bailey Aldrich
Thomas Bulfinch
Thomas De Quincey
Thomas H. Huxley
Thomas Hardy
Thomas More
Thornton W. Burgess
U. S. Grant
Valentine Williams
Victor Appleton
Virginia Woolf
Walter Scott
Washington Irving
Wilbur Lawton
Wilkie Collins
Willa Cather
Willard F. Baker
William Makepeace
Thackeray
William W. Walter
Winston Churchill
Yei Theodora Ozaki
Young E. Allison
Zane Grey